TROPICAL NIGHTS

Tracy Barnes has a few words for real-estate mogul Gregory Thompson. Infuriating. Obstinate. Presumptuous. He's bought the Hawaiian hotel where she works as assistant manager and she could be forced out of her job. If it wasn't for his charm she'd hate him. But Gregory, confident in his ability to win over the guarded Tracy, plans dinner, dancing, and a moonlit walk. Maybe it's Hawaii, but Gregory hasn't felt this good in years . . . or wanted a woman this badly . . .

Books by Phyllis Humphrey
in the Linford Romance Library:

FALSE PRETENCES

PHYLLIS HUMPHREY

TROPICAL NIGHTS

Complete and Unabridged

LINFORD
Leicester

First published in
the United States of America in 2000

First Linford Edition
published 2010

British Library CIP Data

Humphrey, Phyllis A.
  Tropical nights. - -
  (Linford romance library)
  1. Love stories.
  2. Large type books.
  I. Title II. Series
  813.6–dc22

  ISBN 978–1–44480–110–1

Published by
F. A. Thorpe (Publishing)
Anstey, Leicestershire

Set by Words & Graphics Ltd.
Anstey, Leicestershire
Printed and bound in Great Britain by
T. J. International Ltd., Padstow, Cornwall

This book is printed on acid-free paper

1

Tracy Barnes leaned against the tug-boat railing and let her gaze sweep briefly over the brightly dressed passengers that crowded the rail on the deck of the cruise ship. At precisely the moment the tug-boat bumped lightly against the gleaming white bulk of the ship, she saw one face stand out from the rest. A man, taller by far than anyone near him, seemed to be staring directly at her. Even at this distance his looks were arresting: not classically handsome, but rugged in an exciting way. In fact, he reminded her of someone, but his obvious study of her made her uncomfortable, and she turned away before she could make the connection.

'See anyone interesting?' Madeline Hoff called from her seat on the wooden bench that butted against the

1

tug's wheelhouse. Like Tracy, she'd taken the tug from Honolulu harbor to where the cruise ship waited off Diamond Head. Soon they'd board the larger vessel to greet arriving passengers and hand out flower leis of orchid, ginger, and plumeria.

Tracy shrugged, sweeping her shoulder-length blond hair away from her face. 'They look . . . like the usual tourists.' Although she deliberately made no mention of the man whose gaze had locked with hers, impulsively she glanced again at the rail of the cruise ship. But the place he'd occupied was now filled by a gentleman of less height and considerably more girth than his predecessor.

Madeline rose and came to stand beside Tracy. Both were tall and slender, but at five-feet eight, Madeline stood two inches taller.

'Just the usual,' she mimicked good-naturedly. 'Is that a euphemism they use for 'dull' back in Chicago?'

'Chicago?' Tracy said, picking up her

own clear plastic bag of flower leis. 'Isn't that in another galaxy?'

Madeline laughed, her short, dark curls jiggling. 'You should hear yourself. And after only three months in Hawaii. Don't you feel the least bit guilty?'

'Hardly. It's probably snowing there right now.' Tracy watched the two-man crew finish securing the tug, and with practiced ease, as if she'd made this run forty times instead of only four, she stepped over the side and into the wide doorway of the enormous ship at their side.

No, she thought, as she navigated the narrow steps up to the A Deck, she would never miss Chicago, although it represented home, college, and, even before graduation, her first job with Westphal Associates. In her seven years with the company's Lakeside Hotel, she had worked her way up to assistant manager. If it hadn't been for Paul McCandless, she would probably be there still, instead of at their only Hawaiian property.

Paul. She'd finally reached the point where she could think about him without bitterness. The opening for an assistant manager at the Ocean Breeze in Hawaii had appeared shortly after her breakup with him. At twenty-six, it had not been easy starting over; but she loved her job and adored Hawaii. She could, at least, thank him for that.

'I hope you never lose your enthusiasm for the islands,' Madeline said, following Tracy up the stairs to the main salon. 'Or the hotel business, either, which, as we all know, blows like the wind. Hot one minute, cool the next.'

At Madeline's reminder, Tracy frowned. Had she traded one disappointment for another? Only last week, Bill Griffin, the manager, told her about the possibility of the Ocean Breeze Hotel being sold to a real estate consortium. Their representative, a Mr. Gregory Thompson, was due to arrive the next day on the five o'clock flight from Los Angeles.

Tracy's frown deepened. As a member of the staff, she would treat Mr. Thompson with the utmost courtesy. However, that didn't mean she had to like him. Suspecting that if the hotel were sold there'd be more than a good chance she'd be replaced, she had already developed a distaste for the man, sight unseen.

Traversing the deck, Tracy entered the main salon, furnished only with a handful of tables holding large signs neatly lettered in blue. She found the one reserved for the Ocean Breeze, and, unfastening the ties that closed one of the plastic bags, let the leis tumble out onto the table. They were still damp, and she lifted and shook them gently, scattering tiny drops of dew that soon evaporated in the warm air.

Then, abruptly, she stopped. An odd sensation came over her; she was being watched. She looked up and found the same man who had caught her eye earlier. As he approached the table, she could see that his face and neck were deeply tanned above the crisp blue collar of his shirt; that, besides dark wavy hair, he had a straight nose and square-cut jaw with a distinct and very attractive cleft in his chin. Now she knew who he reminded her of. Except that he didn't have a mustache, and appeared to be in his mid-thirties, he resembled the star of a television series about a private detective.

A shadow came between her and the light and suddenly he was at the table. Tracy stared. My God, she thought, he's a giant. He must be six feet four. But of course she wasn't wearing heels today. Then she noticed the unabashed way in which he returned her stare and the open expression on his face that made it obvious he was doing some thinking about her as well. Unnerved, she cleared her throat and prepared to deliver the routine speech with which she always welcomed guests of the hotel.

'Welcome to Hawaii.' She said it briskly, professionally, setting the stage for business. 'May I give you a lei?'

Her last few words hung in the air between them, little leaden words that dropped with an embarrassing thud, and Tracy cringed inwardly.

However, before this particular man had time to do any more than curve his lips into a slow-spreading grin, she said, 'That didn't come out at all the way I'd planned. Why don't I start again?'

'It sounded fine to me,' he offered in a pleasantly deep voice. 'But if you think you can improve on it I'm game.'

She wondered if he were patronizing her, of if the words were meant to restore her confidence. She glanced up into warm, brown eyes. His look seemed sincere enough.

She took a deep breath. 'Welcome to Hawaii,' she began. 'Would you like — ' Again she stopped, thoroughly annoyed at her inability to make the greeting sound anything but X-rated.

'I most certainly would.' His gaze swept the length of her body before returning to her face. His eyes, she

7

noted, had tiny gold flecks that seemed to dance within the irises. Also, he made no pretense of concealing his amusement.

'Believe it or not,' Tracy said, finding it easier at the moment to address the ginger lei she held in her hands than this very tall, very disturbing man who hovered above her, 'I've delivered this speech at least fifty times in the past three months and usually with a lot more finesse.'

Regaining something of her poise, she glanced up. 'However, since that doesn't seem to be the case this morning, would you mind very much if we skipped the preliminaries?' With any luck at all, he would take the flower lei and go back out on deck. If he stayed in here any longer, he'd completely short-circuit her thought processes.

His smile held more than a hint of mischief. 'Ah, but if we were to do that — ' He shrugged.

His shoulders, she could hardly help noticing, were nicely proportioned. She

8

wondered if he worked out a lot, or jogged. He had a noticeably athletic body.

' — you would have to forfeit something, or at least make it up in some other way.'

'Oh?' She didn't need any mixed signals this morning and certainly not from him.

'Perhaps we could stop for coffee,' he suggested, 'on the way to the hotel. Then we could begin to get to know one another. I can't think of a better welcome to Hawaii than that.'

Well, that signal was clear enough. Attractive or not, the man was a perfect stranger, and a guest of the hotel. 'I'm sorry,' she said. 'I won't be going with you to the Ocean Breeze.'

'You won't?' His disappointment was unmistakable.

'You have to claim your luggage,' she said, 'and turn in those pesky forms the state provides. Sometimes it takes a while.'

That seemed to amuse him, because

he grinned. 'And you won't wait?' He cocked his head sideways, sending a loose lock of thick, brown hair over his forehead.

Surprisingly, everything about the man made Tracy wish it were otherwise. But, after a pause, she said firmly, 'I can't.'

'I thought a good hotel did everything to accommodate its guests. You know, roll out the red carpet, bring on a brass band, hold your hand while you claim your luggage.'

'You don't want much.' She laughed, giving him high marks for persistence, as well as a king-size measure of charm and humor. At the same time a red flag went up in the back of her mind; he was too much. 'We do what we can, within reason, that is. And there are rules — '

'I thought those were meant to be broken.' His expression turned serious, but his eyes, Tracy noticed, were soft and warm, and sparkled with suppressed laughter.

'Not this time.'

'Perhaps bent a little?' He panto-mimed with his hands.

'No,' she said firmly. It wasn't a mere rule that checked her. She knew her sudden attraction to him was strong enough to indeed bend rules. She'd bent a similar rule for Paul, even though she had always thought it foolish to date coworkers. She'd promised herself not to do anything like that again.

He seemed to accept her refusal. 'Do you go back to Honolulu on the tug?'

'No,' Tracy answered, 'we dock with the ship. The pilot's aboard now and he'll guide us into the harbor.' She pointed to the slowly moving view of Diamond Head outside the windows. 'We're on our way now.'

'So we are.'

As his gaze turned toward the open sea, Tracy covertly studied his face. His broad forehead and high cheekbones suggested intelligence and strength, that he was very much his own man. But it was his well-shaped, sensuous lips, and dark eyes that reminded her of soft velvet, that gave him a very human quality and made her pulse race.

'Tell me,' he asked, turning to her again, 'is this what you do primarily for the hotel, ride out on tugboats to greet the guests?'

'That's the least of it,' she said. 'I'm the assistant manager of the Ocean Breeze. You could say I do a little bit of everything, but coming out here to meet the guests is one part of my job I especially enjoy.'

'Mmm. Me, too.' The side of his mouth curled up in a lopsided grin, and Tracy's heart did a roller-coaster drop. 'And are you good at what you do, that little bit of everything?'

'You won't have any complaints,' Tracy assured him, taking refuge in shop talk to quell her sensations. 'The hotel is very well run; the staff, from Bill Griffin, the manager, on down, are very efficient. We all work as hard as if we owned the place.'

'Is that what you'd like to do

someday, own a hotel?'

The question took her by surprise. 'I'd like very much to manage one,' she admitted. 'But to own a hotel, no. It sounds exciting and glamorous, but there are too many pitfalls.'

She thought of Madeline Hoff, who owned the Island Sands. She'd had to trim the staff to the bone, and for the past two months had been operating without an assistant. Poor Madeline, Tracy thought; the obvious stress she was under was beginning to mar her youthful good looks.

'Still,' he was saying, 'people brave those pitfalls every day. If not, there'd be no Hiltons or Sheratons or — '

'Please,' Tracy admonished with a laugh. 'We never mention the competition around here. It's strictly forbidden.'

'In that case, I give you my word their names will never pass my lips again. Shall we shake on it?' He held out his hand, inviting Tracy to slip hers into it.

She hesitated a moment, caught

between the desire to be touched, even so briefly, by him, and her natural instinct that warned her to be wary of a man who already had such an effect on her. Then the moment passed. Tracy gave him her hand, feeling the strength in the fingers closing around hers.

'This makes us conspirators,' he said.

Reluctantly, she let her common sense return and slid her hand from his warm grasp.

'Well,' she said briskly, 'I trust you'll enjoy your stay in Hawaii.' There was a conclusive ring to her words and she supposed that now he would leave the salon. And didn't she have mixed feelings about that?

'Aren't you forgetting something?' he asked casually, and that same spark of mischief flared in his eyes.

'Forgetting?'

'If we can't have coffee together, I'll almost have to insist on the lei you promised.'

He would remember that, Tracy thought. But, to his credit, the way he

14

worded the request made it sound, if not totally innocuous, then at least only mildly suggestive. With a sigh of resignation, she picked up a lei strung with ginger blossoms and handed it to him.

He glanced at the strand of delicate flowers linked together in a circlet, their heady, perfumed scent filling the air around them. With a surprisingly light touch, he fingered the pearly-white petals, suggesting to Tracy that those strong hands could be gentle as well.

'Aren't you going to put it around my neck?' The seductively deep timbre of his voice made Tracy's gaze move upward to meet his. Briefly, the intensity of his stare held her motionless; then, somehow, she found herself moving around the table toward him, her pulse beating rapidly in her throat, her hands warm with sudden perspiration.

He moved closer, inclining his head. Still, he was so tall — and she felt suddenly too short in her flat sandals

— that Tracy had to stretch on her tiptoes to put the lei over his bowed head and onto his shoulders. Then, her heart racing, she gave him a peck on first one cheek and then the other, her nostrils filling with the pungent aroma of the flowers and the refreshingly cool scent of his cologne.

'The aloha greeting,' he murmured, with a grin that managed to be both innocent and sexy at the same time, 'needs a little more warmth. May I show you?'

Before Tracy could answer, he picked up a pikake lei and placed it around her neck over her sleeveless flower-print dress. His warm hands on her bare shoulders, he bent to her upturned face. Bringing his lips to her cheeks, he kissed each slowly, deliberately, as if tasting some sweet nectar that lingered there.

In an instant, Tracy felt as if the air were charged with an electric current. In spite of acknowledging the intensity of the attraction that had been building

16

from the start, she pulled away. She would put a stop to that, she told herself, and the sooner the better.

She turned away from him, but he drew her back, seemingly oblivious to the dozens of people who milled about the salon. He raised his hands from her shoulders to the sides of her face, and this time his lips descended on hers. They were firm and cool and for a brief moment her own clung to them willingly.

Her eyes closed automatically at his kiss, then good sense overruled her emotions and they flew open. She pushed him away. 'That,' she informed him firmly, 'is *not* the way it's done.'

'But my way is more fun,' he said, 'especially when, as in this case, the recipient is so attractive.'

'The aloha greeting, in this case,' Tracy stressed, 'is strictly business.' She looked at him in what she hoped was a cold, aloof manner. Yet her hands, her face, her entire body, felt anything but cold.

'I'm sorry to hear it,' he said easily. 'Maybe I'll change your mind about that sometime.'

Tracy nervously fingered the leis that remained on the table. 'It would hardly be worth the effort.'

His gaze was provocative, his eyes frankly and pleasantly appraising as they traveled down her body. 'Since I'm staying at your hotel,' he said softly, 'I expect we'll be seeing a lot of each other.'

'I wouldn't allow my expectations to get too high,' she said, her lips feeling tight. 'The management seldom mingles with the guests.'

He laughed deeply. 'Not permitted to fraternize?'

'Something like that,' Tracy said. This was no rule, but good sound judgment. Lasting relationships — the only kind she wanted — were not forged by becoming involved with hotel guests. They were, after all, tourists and business people, whose stay rarely lasted more than a week or two. No electricity, no chemistry, between them — and, God help her, this was stronger than anything she had ever felt before — could overcome her natural instinct that such a relationship contained a built-in destruct mechanism.

In spite of her coolness, his smile remained open and friendly, his voice teasingly warm. 'Now that we've become so well acquainted' — he emphasized the last two words, then paused — 'don't you think it's about time you told me your name?'

'I'm Tracy Barnes,' she managed to say.

'What a lovely name; it suits a very lovely lady. I'll look forward to seeing you again, Miss Barnes. Until then, aloha.' With a parting smile, he turned and left the salon.

Staring at his retreating back, Tracy thought, *Oh, no, you won't.*

So what if she was terribly attracted to him — his kiss had sent her blood pressure soaring — nevertheless, she wouldn't let herself get involved. The

Ocean Breeze was not a very large hotel — only four stories high — and most of her work was done in the office behind the lobby. If she wished, she could avoid him quite easily; and, she told herself, that's exactly what she'd do.

2

As more passengers approached her table in the salon of the cruise ship — they seemed to come in a sudden rush, as if the man she'd just spoken to had somehow programmed them to remain in the background until he left — Tracy pushed aside her thoughts of that unsettling kiss. Smiling pleasantly, she went about the business of slipping the fragrant leis over the shoulders of the men and women who were booked into the Ocean Breeze. However, her thoughts refused to concentrate on the task, and she found herself merely going through the motions. Finally, every lei was distributed, except one, the circle of three strands of tiny white pikake blossoms around her own neck.

I'll keep them as a reminder — no, a warning, she thought. She left the salon and made her way through the

21

passengers, descending past the swimming pool and shuffleboard court to the lower deck. She didn't see the man again, and, relieved, she found a position at the forward rail. From there, she watched the ship maneuver into the harbor toward the dock. Although it was barely nine o'clock, the sun was high, the air warm and filled with the fragrance of tropical blooms that mingled with the strong scent of salt sea air. Sun-bronzed children swam about the slowly moving vessel, shouting for the passengers to throw coins. It was a ritual that Tracy enjoyed; and, reaching into her purse for some loose change, she tossed it to the children, who dove expertly for it.

Finally, the gap between pier and ship narrowed, and Tracy found herself caught in a hail of paper streamers which had been given out to the passengers earlier. The ship, the dock, virtually everything in sight, suddenly turned into a kaleidoscope of reds, greens, yellows and blues, as friends and relatives waiting below caught the ends of the bright streamers. Tracy imagined the ship tied to the land by the colorful thin strips of paper, rather than by the heavy ropes.

Then the band, twenty well-tanned men in a uniform of white trousers and red jackets, struck up a lively tune; and Madeline Hoff appeared out of the crowd and came toward her. 'Are you ready to go?'

'Yes.' Tracy followed the other woman down several flights of narrow stairs until they emerged near a gangplank where the crew members could disembark. A light breeze caught the hem of Tracy's cotton print dress, billowing it out around her bare legs.

'Tell me,' Madeline said, as they joined the end of the line waiting to leave the ship, 'who was that attractive man who took up so much of your time? The very tall, conveniently young one,' she added with a playful glint in her eye.

Tracy stopped and took a deep

breath. Was it possible they had spoken for so long, even kissed, and yet he had never told her his name? 'Just another guest of the hotel,' she said at last.

'Ah, would that all hotel guests were as handsome,' Madeline remarked. 'My establishment seems to attract mostly senior citizens. As in slow, stooped and shuffling.'

'But you have something much better than a handsome guest,' Tracy said. 'You have Bill, who is not only young and good-looking too but, unlike guests, is not about to go back to the mainland without you.' Madeline and the manager of the Ocean Breeze had been dating since before Tracy had come to work in the Islands.

'That's true, but he told me that your hotel might be sold and he'd be out of a job.'

'Let's not cross that bridge before we come to it.'

'But aren't you coming to it soon?' Madeline asked. 'Bill told me that a representative from some big hotel chain is coming to check it out for that very purpose. Bill said he's arriving tomorrow and will be getting the red carpet treatment.'

'He's paying for it,' Tracy said. 'Well, figuratively, anyway. If his company buys the hotel, the carpet will go right along with it.' She hadn't meant to sound bitter, but there it was anyway. 'My job as well. If they buy the Breeze, it's almost certain I'll be out. Bill's position is probably much more secure. Good managers are hard to find.'

'Assistant managers too,' Madeline said. 'You're very good at what you do. Bill comments on it often.'

Tracy didn't want to elaborate, but it had been her experience that, when a hotel changed hands, the new owners brought in their own top level personnel. It had prompted her, the week before, to do some discreet checking through a friend in the Chicago office. Unfortunately, there were no openings at the moment for assistant managers in any of the Westphal hotels. That meant if she lost her job, she would have to start again, resumé in hand, if she still wanted a career in this business. Worst of all, it would push back by years her goal to become manager of a really fine, first-class hotel.

'Are you that concerned?' Madeline asked as they walked down the gangplank, watching a covey of taxi drivers waiting for passengers.

For her sake, Tracy tried to make light of the situation. 'Maybe I'm just being overly cautious.'

'I'd offer you a job at the Sands,' Madeline volunteered, 'except I'm doing them all myself.' She laughed.

Tracy knew that the Island Sands had not shown a profit for some time and she felt genuinely sorry for Madeline, who was barely hanging on to it.

'Or I suppose you could go back to Chicago,' Madeline continued. 'But I'd sure miss you.'

Tracy couldn't help an ironic smile. That had been the subject of their conversation on the way to the ship this morning, and now it had surfaced again. 'I'd miss you too; but don't worry, Chicago is out of the question.' No, even if there were a good job there, she would not return to that city. Though she was certain she was finally over Paul, she wanted no reminders.

Instead, the lei, emitting a sweet fragrance as she touched the satiny petals, reminded her of the man who had placed the string of flowers around her neck. Then her hands stole to her cheeks, where he'd touched her. A sudden warmth that was more than the tropical air suffused her body.

★   ★   ★

When Tracy returned to the Ocean Breeze, she went directly to her apartment, a two-room suite on the ground floor, facing a lush, well-tended tropical garden.

She liked to think of the apartment as her cocoon, a small insular haven to which she could escape when she needed some quiet time. It reflected her own taste, which Tracy had always thought of jokingly as midwestern cosmopolitan, a cross between brass and glass and thick pile and cushioned comfort. However, in Hawaii, she had to make do with the hotel's furnishings. She looked around at the non-descript beige couch and imitation teakwood table, to which she had added prints by island artists Guy Buffet and Pegge Hopper, a hand-doweled beech-wood rocker that had belonged to her great grandmother, and a collection of cut-glass owls of varying sizes that had arrived, miraculously, without a chip.

She opened the folding louvered doors which separated the kitchen from the living room and poured herself a glass of orange juice, then sank onto the couch and leaned into the jumble of bright pillows that lay heaped in the corner. Work beckoned, but for once she ignored its summons. Her body felt limp, her mind refusing to focus on the myriad duties that awaited her in her office. Today, her mental capacity seemed diminished, her concentration a fragile bubble ready to burst at the slightest provocation. And she knew why; it was the fault of the man she'd met on the ship. Where she should have been thinking of checkout times and linen quotas, she had a clear image of flashing brown eyes and the touch of warm, strong hands that had made her heart leap into her throat.

Almost an hour had passed since she'd left him aboard the cruise ship, but she was as acutely aware of his touch now as she had been then. She would have liked more time alone to sort out the matter, to find some rational explanation for her lingering awareness of him. Like a sorcerer, she thought, touching a finger to her lips where he had planted that brief kiss, he had managed to cast one heck of a spell on her. But at least she knew the antidote. She'd stay out of his way, let the tropical breeze and perfume-scented nights work their magic on some other woman.

That settled, at least for the time being, Tracy finished her juice, then pushed herself up from the couch with an admonition to go out and earn her daily bread. In her bedroom, where her own touches consisted of an Oriental silkscreen and a vivid blue and white quilted spread on the double bed, she slipped into a fresh lightweight dress in shades of pink and higher-heeled shoes than she'd worn for the trip on the tug that morning. Then she stepped out of her apartment.

The office area behind the lobby of the hotel reminded Tracy of a rabbit warren: six small rooms, some with no immediate access to a short, narrow hallway, except through other rooms. Her own office was centrally located and cluttered with the mountain of paper that went along with running a successful one hundred and twenty-five room hotel.

She sat down at her desk just as Bill Griffin came through the door that connected his and Tracy's offices.

'Do you have a minute? There's something I'd like to discuss with you.' Bill, whose pleasant disposition made him a delight to work with, jammed his hands deep into the pockets of his trousers and returned to his own quarters.

Following him into the larger room, Tracy noted the serious tone, the unaccustomed reserve in the ordinarily candid hazel eyes. Had something gone wrong at the hotel? Or, worse, had news of the highly unorthodox aloha greeting from the man on the ship reached him already?

'I have some good news for you,' Bill said. 'You're going to be the next manager of the Ocean Breeze Hotel.'

'That'll be the day!' But something about his grin caused her stomach to tighten. Her mouth fell open. 'You've got to be kidding. You are kidding, aren't you? I don't believe it. When did it happen? *How* did it happen?'

'Wait a minute, one question at a time. I didn't want to drop it in your lap this way, but my letter of resignation to Mr. Westphal will be in the mail this afternoon.'

'You're resigning? Why?'

'I almost made this move five months ago, but before I had a chance, my assistant Ellen quit. Then it took a couple of weeks for you to get out here, and of course I couldn't just go off and leave you to fend for yourself.'

Tracy grinned. 'Believe me, I appreciate that.'

'And you've been a godsend.' Bill pushed a lock of unruly sandy hair away from his brow. 'Another month or so and Madeline would be a candidate for the funny farm.'

'Madeline?' He was going too fast for her. Either that or she was particularly dense today.

Bill perched on the edge of the desk and leaned toward Tracy. 'Madeline and I are going into business together.

Well, she's already in business. I'll be joining her, as a partner.'

'At the Island Sands?' Tracy began getting ominous thoughts. By Bill's own account, Madeline's hotel had been losing money steadily.

'A rich old aunt of mine died six months ago and left me some money, a lot more than I expected. Madeline and I intend to have a short engagement, probably one of the shortest in history,' he added with a laugh, 'then get married and put all our energies and my new resources into the hotel.'

So that was why Madeline seemed so unconcerned about Bill being displaced if the Breeze were sold to that chain. He'd be long gone before the new owners got around to serving any pink slips. Only she, Tracy, would be there, hand out, bags packed, future uncertain. Have experience, will travel. Now, if only she had a fiancé on the horizon who just happened to own a hotel! A solvent fiancé, of course.

Tracy smiled at her soon-to-be

former boss. At least his future looked bright. 'Congratulations.'

'Thanks. I'm one lucky guy, what with Madeline *and* enough money to pay off bills and spruce up the Island Sands.'

'That's wonderful. I know you'll be successful.'

'And now,' Bill announced, 'that brings us to you. This,' he said, with mock solemnity, 'will be all yours in two weeks. In my letter to Mr. Westphal, I recommended that he promote you to high honcho around here. In my book, you're the best thing that could happen to any hotel.'

'I don't know what to say,' Tracy murmured, deeply touched by his confidence in her and his thoughtfulness. It made her realize what a good friend Bill had become in so short a time. It was ironic, though, coming as it did, just when that hotel conglomerate might be about to snatch it away from her.

Bill gave her a thumbs-up sign.

'Don't say anything until we hear from the main office.'

'But what about that Titan Industries' representative who's supposed to show up tomorrow?'

He paused before continuing. 'What I said before still goes. If they have any sense at all, you'll be in.'

'Except it might be out of Westphal's hands by then,' Tracy said. 'Unless, of course, he decides against selling the hotel.'

'Or,' Bill added, 'if for some reason, it doesn't measure up to Gregory Thompson's expectations, and his company declines to buy it.'

'One can but hope.' Barring that, Tracy thought, there was always the possibility that someone, perhaps a certain assistant manager, might slip some arsenic into Mr. Thompson's mai tai!

She smiled at the crazy idea, just as someone knocked on the office door. Bill went to open it.

As it opened, Tracy looked toward

the door. Standing on the threshold was a tall, handsome man. Not just any tall, handsome man, but the same one Tracy had met only this morning on the cruise ship. The one who had kissed her.

'Mr. Griffin?' he said, 'the young lady at the desk told me I'd find you here. I'm Gregory Thompson.'

3

At first, the name meant nothing; then a moment later it registered with full impact. Gregory Thompson — the real estate consortium — the people who might buy the hotel and eliminate her job. Tracy felt her legs go limp.

He came farther into the room, shook hands with Bill. 'Is there something wrong?' he asked then, as if just noticing no one else had spoken.

'No, nothing's wrong,' Bill said. 'We weren't expecting you yet, that's all. This is my assistant, Tracy Barnes.'

He came close and took her hand. 'Miss Barnes and I have already met.'

Tracy mumbled a 'hello,' then turned to Bill. 'On the *Lillesand* this morning,' she said. Her thoughts were flying; why had he come a day early, and on a cruise ship instead of a flight from the mainland?

'Has my arriving like this caused a problem?' he asked.

'We expected you tomorrow,' Bill answered.

'I had a slight change in plans.' He flashed Tracy a brilliant smile. 'Actually, I surprised myself,' he went on. 'That was the first cruise I've ever taken. I'd never had the time before, nor the inclination for that matter. I booked it on the spur of the moment, less than two weeks ago.'

Tracy hardly listened; her indignation soared. He had flirted with her, even kissed her, and all the while he knew — even if she didn't — that his company might buy the hotel, and they, in turn, might hire their own staff and leave her standing in the unemployment line.

'Won't you have a seat?' Bill said.

'If this isn't a convenient time — '

'No, it's all right. We were just finished anyway.'

Tracy took Bill's comment to mean she was excused and headed for the door. Probably they were going to discuss financial matters and perhaps take a tour of the hotel. She smiled and nodded at Bill, but kept her gaze away from Gregory Thompson's face. At the moment, putting arsenic in his mai tai didn't seem such a ridiculous idea after all.

She returned to her office and tried to resume her work, but thoughts of Gregory Thompson intruded. She remembered every moment of their meeting on board the ship, the strong, clean lines of his face, his sensuous lips. Instinctively she had felt his strength, his confidence, his magnetism. But what about now? She felt as if he'd deliberately lied to her, teased and tempted her, never revealing that he wasn't a friend, but an enemy.

She picked up a pencil, then abruptly threw it down. No, she had to be fair. He hadn't lied to her. All right, he had flirted with her, but when had that become a crime? On the other hand, he should have told her who he was the moment she gave him *her* name.

Why hadn't he? Did he just forget, or did he want to conceal it until a later time? And if she hadn't been in Bill's office just now, when would he have gotten around to revealing the real reason for his being in the hotel? No matter how much she was attracted to him physically, she could never become interested in a man who concealed things, who was less than totally up-front and honest at all times.

Her telephone rang, forcing her to push these thoughts aside; but she knew they'd return. Furthermore, the moment the hotel was sold and she lost her job — her first, perhaps, as manager — she'd hate Gregory Thompson.

★ ★ ★

By dusk, Tracy had dealt successfully with a dozen situations, from misplaced storage keys to a snag in the room service routine, proving, at least to her satisfaction, that Bill's confidence in her was not misplaced.

It had been a long day, and she could feel the energy slowly draining from her body as she crossed the smooth, red-tiled patio where several dozen glasstopped tables and cane chairs were arranged around a small dance floor. Open on the sides, the patio was protected only by a conical thatched roof. In the shadows cast by individual candles that sat on each table in etched glass hurricane lamps, and a brilliantly red sinking sun, six couples danced to the soft strains of a five-piece band, while others ordered dinner from a menu featuring favorite island dishes.

'Miss Barnes. So we meet again, after all.'

Startled, Tracy turned back toward the patio. There, smiling at her, as if he had materialized out of the night itself, stood Gregory Thompson, dressed in a light tropical suit and navy blue open-neck shirt.

Tracy shivered. She wished she'd anticipated the moment, rehearsed what she'd say to him. Should she smile and treat him like any other hotel guest, confront him angrily, or just turn away in scorn? Which?

'Mr. Thompson.' She nodded coolly in his direction. Perhaps professionalism was the best way to handle this. 'Are you enjoying your stay?'

'My room is comfortable and I've had an excellent dinner.' In two long strides he was standing beside her on the flagstone path, where misty pools of light spilled from the tiki torches bordering the garden. 'I was just about to have a cognac. Could I persuade you to join me this time?'

Tracy glanced up at his face. Its planes seemed more pronounced in the fading light. His eyes bored into hers, beckoning her, not with a plea, but with assurance.

Oh, no you don't, Mr. Thompson, she thought, her every nerve sensing immediate danger.

'I'm sorry, but that's not possible.' Her tone — brisk, impersonal —

implied she had more important things to do. 'But don't let me keep you from enjoying your drink.'

'I'd enjoy it a lot more if I had company.' He grinned down at her with a cajoling expression that seemed calculated to melt even the most hardened resistance. 'You see, I have a theory about cognac. It never tastes its best unless accompanied by good conversation and charming company.'

Now he was trying to flatter her. And why not? Women were notorious for falling for that old ploy.

She looked directly into his eyes. 'How interesting,' she said in a voice that was far steadier than her pulse. 'I've never heard that one before. How long have you had this theory?'

He knit his brows. 'Oh, about five minutes, I'd say.'

Tracy barely suppressed a laugh. Once more his humor was managing to dissipate her anger. 'At least you're honest.'

'Theories, I find, are like new

relationships,' he went on, encouraged apparently by her continuing to stand there. His gaze swept across her face and down her throat. 'Too often, they're kept on the back burner when, in fact, they should be put to the test immediately. Don't you agree?'

Tracy glanced sideways. Finally she answered his question. 'I don't drink cognac, Mr. Thompson, so I can't help you prove your theory.' She gestured with a light airy motion toward the patio. 'But there must be any number of people still in the restaurant eager to engage you in conversation.' She took a step away. 'Now I really must say good night.'

She walked toward the swimming pool, flanked on one side by webbed lounge chairs, and on the other by several round glass tables topped with umbrellas.

'The point is,' he went on, catching up to her and matching the length of his stride to hers, 'one must talk to the right person for exciting conversation.'

Tracy studied his face for a sign that he was playing games with her. 'You seem to be going out of your way to flatter me, Mr. Thompson.'

'If being honest about wanting someone's company is flattery, then, yes, I'm flattering you.' He looked at her with an open, sincere expression, his voice husky, threatening to undo Tracy's composure. 'By the way, are you going to continue calling me Mr. Thompson?' he asked in a gentle tone, 'or do you think you could try Greg?'

'I'm sorry, but you're a guest of the hotel.' She paused, made a decision. 'You spoke of honesty just now, so let me be honest with you. It's entirely possible you may be instrumental in my losing my job. That, together with the way you behaved this morning, is reason enough for me to want to keep our relationship on a strictly business level.' The long speech had taken her breath away and she inhaled deeply. She moved around the pool, where pale lights shimmered under the calm surface.

He followed closely. 'I seem to have made a bad first impression. I'm truly sorry for whatever I did or said that offended you this morning. But I assure you I'm not your enemy, although you seem to think I am.'

'You're here to look over the Ocean Breeze and if you recommend that your company buy it, I could well be out of a job. That doesn't make you out to be a friend, does it?'

'I merely represent Titan Industries. I'm sorry if that creates a problem for you; but it's hardly my fault.'

Tracy knew he was right, and his charming apology had all but destroyed her antagonism. At least she could be civil. 'What exactly does Titan Industries do, besides purchase hotels?'

'We buy raw land and build on it. And, of course, we buy and develop existing properties. Mostly hotels, but we have several office complexes in Los Angeles and one or two high rises in major cities.' He gave her a half smile. 'Don't tell me you didn't know all that.'

Tracy watched the pink stucco buildings catch the last crimson rays of the sun. The sky had turned darker and a perfectly full moon rose to spill its pale light on the earth. 'And now you're going to buy this hotel?'

Greg made a grimace. 'Not necessarily. Perhaps I don't like your hotel. Perhaps I don't share your enthusiasm for the Islands.'

'Really?' Tracy asked, surprised. 'You don't like Hawaii?'

'I've never been here before. Someone told me it's a lot like Mexico. I know something about that. I spent almost a year commuting between Los Angeles and Yucatan. The temperature never dropped out of the nineties, the bugs were so big you could throw a saddle on them, and I learned to identify no less than five different varieties of snake.' He laughed. 'If I sound like I'm complaining, I am.'

'But Hawaii isn't a bit like Mexico,'

Tracy said. She held up her fingers one at a time. 'First, you speak the language; second, you can understand the money; third, it's safe to drink the water; and, fourth, there are no snakes in Hawaii.'

'Spoken like a member of the Chamber of Commerce.'

Tracy found herself smiling. 'Touché.' She paused, then added, 'I didn't mean to make light of your experience. It must have been very unpleasant.'

'It was, but someone had to do it,' Greg continued. 'We bought an old hotel down there. The place was almost in the jungle. Believe me, in the end, it came down to man against nature, and nature almost won.'

She caught a glimpse of his tall, sturdily built body through the corner of her eye. Everything about Greg Thompson radiated strength and power. She almost imagined he could battle the jungles of Mexico with one hand wrapped around a cold marguerita.

'It took two years to complete the

project, and we ran a million and a half over budget.'

'What hotel did you buy?' she asked.

'The Monarch, although it doesn't go by that now. We renamed it La Casa Grande.'

Tracy stopped short, almost colliding with him. 'La Casa Grande, that utter monstrosity of glass towers and misplaced turrets?' She recalled the arcades crammed with shops that sold everything from plastic palm trees to designer bikinis. There had been jungle, all right, but it had been hacked and chopped and obliterated until you could barely see the trees for the concrete they had poured in there. That was where the extra million and a half must have gone!

'You've seen the project?' he asked.

'Unfortunately, yes.'

'Let me guess. You don't approve.'

His facetious remark was said with a grin, and she was charmed again by his lighthearted attitude. But how could he have had anything to do with that

49

grotesque excuse for a hotel? Had she been mistaken about his sensitivity?

'I'm sorry if you're insulted,' she said more harshly than she intended, totally negating the apology.

Undoing the single button, he opened his jacket. 'You're entitled to your opinion,' he said, with no hint of offense. 'Aside from the turrets, would you mind telling me what you dislike about it?'

Tracy groaned. 'Do you have all night?'

'Yes.' His voice lowered and in an instant he had changed her innocent remark into something totally different.

She ignored the innuendo. 'In the first place, it doesn't take its setting into consideration. Instead of blending in, being in harmony with nature, it — ' She didn't know how to express herself tactfully, so she took a deep breath and just let it come out. 'It's just plain awful.'

He held up his hands as if warding off an assailant. 'You don't pull your punches, do you?'

'I find it hard to imagine how you could have had a hand in building something so ugly. To anyone who has the slightest appreciation for the environment, it's pillage and rape!'

That had been her first thought two years before, when she had seen La Casa Grande on a vacation to Mexico. And, in spite of the man who now stood with her in the moonlight, she was not about to change her mind.

He thrust one hand into his pocket, and made a palms-up gesture with the other. 'The project took hits from a dozen different sides, but not even the nature lovers in Mexico and the United States condemned it to *that* degree.'

'I'm sorry,' she apologized again. It was totally unlike her to be rude to anyone. 'I shouldn't have gotten so — so — ' She searched for the right word. None would come.

'Passionate?' he filled in. 'I don't mind.' His tone changed; he was back in his seductive mode.

Tracy felt a surge of emotion. She didn't at all care to think about passion, and would have told him so if his eyes hadn't taken on such a sparkle and the moonlight hadn't turned his hair blacker than a nighthawk's wing.

For a while, neither spoke, as if both were aware of the subtle change that had taken place in their relationship. Then, struggling to return to the subject, although her animosity over his part in the Casa Grande fiasco had dwindled, Tracy said, 'Is that what you're going to do to the Ocean Breeze?'

She gazed about the grounds. Though it was night, her imagination pictured it by day, the gazebo flanked by crimson hibiscus, purple bougainvillea hanging from latticed overhead beams, palm trees offering shade from the tropical sun. All that would be gone, replaced by brick and stone, glass and steel.

'I'm not going to do anything to the Ocean Breeze,' she heard Greg say. 'As

I explained to Bill Griffin this afternoon, my job is to investigate properties and, if both sides are interested, to reach an agreement with the present owners. Your hotel is not the only one under consideration. I have over a dozen to see before I leave the South Pacific.' He paused. 'I'm flying to Fiji tomorrow or the day after. Come with me.'

Travel to Fiji with him? Greg Thompson really was a fast worker.

'Or I can postpone it if that's more convenient for you.'

'Don't be ridiculous.' Tracy shook her head and changed the subject. 'Do you enjoy your work?'

He stopped walking. They'd reached the end of the garden path where a wall of lava rock stretched out before them. 'I do most of the time. It depends on the project. Then again, it's the kind of work that can take up twenty-six hours of your day if you let it.'

'And do you?'

He shrugged. 'My wife thought I did.

That's why she divorced me two years ago.'

Tracy realized suddenly that she hadn't given the slightest thought to the fact that he might be married.

'I'm sorry about your divorce,' she said. Only, she didn't feel in the least sorry. She felt vastly relieved, then shocked at her reaction. *He's not for you*, she reminded herself.

'So was I at the time. But, of course, Sally was right. The business took everything, my time, energy, imagination. That left damn little to give to a marriage. In short, I made a lousy husband. The breakup was entirely my own fault.'

Tracy admired his honesty and yet she couldn't help wondering if his speech contained a broad hint. *I'm very attracted to you, Tracy*, he might be thinking, *and I'd like to pursue that while I'm here in your island paradise, but I'm not very good husband material, so don't get any permanent ideas.*

She glanced across the few feet of space that separated them. If only she could read his thoughts — perhaps they would mirror the open sincerity in his look.

But why bother wasting time and energy even wondering about Greg Thompson's thoughts? He was just passing through her world, stopping off only so briefly. She had no intention of starting anything with him, not a relationship, and certainly not a one-, two-, or five-night stand. So, if she had any sense at all, she would say good night now, and if she were smart she would say good-bye.

Instead, she said neither.

'Have you ever been married?' he asked suddenly, moving closer to her.

'No.'

'Ever come close?'

She hated to think about her two years with Paul, his wanting their involvement to go on and on, his not understanding that their relationship had reached a crossroads.

But Greg was waiting for an answer, and she found herself saying, 'I thought so, once.'

'What happened?' he asked, his tone barely above a whisper.

Tracy gave a short laugh. For a brief second she considered telling him that she'd been hurt badly, but changed her mind. 'Nothing happened,' she said honestly.

'He was a fool.'

The words seemed to have a double effect on her. First, she heartily agreed that Paul had been a fool to let her go; but then the hurt of their parting returned and she felt vulnerable. Tears stinging her eyes, she turned away and began to walk quickly toward the hotel. 'Good night.'

As if surprised by her sudden departure, Greg didn't say anything at all or move to follow her. She told herself she didn't want him to follow her, didn't want to see him again. Or did she?

4

Tracy tried to push Greg Thompson out of her thoughts; but he kept returning, like a song you've heard that keeps repeating itself in your brain, long after you wish you could think of something else.

The truth was, she liked him. Something had clicked between them the moment he looked at her from the railing of the cruise ship; and nothing since then — including considering him a threat to her job, if not her peace of mind — could diminish the impact. The more she knew of him, the more she found things to admire. Forget that he was one of the handsomest men she'd ever met. He'd accepted her brutal assessment of La Casa Grande with good grace; he'd admitted his part in the breakup of his marriage; and he seemed genuinely interested in getting to know her better.

Well, perhaps the latter could be considered part of an effort to add a night or two of pleasure to his business trip. She couldn't really fault him for that.

The next afternoon, Bill summoned her into his office. 'I have a favor to ask of you.'

She sat in the chair in front of his desk. 'A favor? Since when are the boss's orders a favor? Of course, I'll do anything you want me to.'

'But this isn't strictly business.' He paused only a moment, before adding, 'Well, technically it is.'

Tracy laughed. 'You're making it sound mysterious.'

'I want you to accompany Gregory Thompson on a short tour of the island.'

Tracy felt her breath catch; this was certainly not what she had expected. 'Why does he need a tour, accompanied at that? He's a grown man: I have no doubt he can find his way around all by himself.'

'It's not my idea,' Bill said, 'it's Westphal's. When he said, 'roll out the red carpet,' he meant it. He phoned this morning and reminded me that whatever Thompson wants, Thompson gets. So — '

'So,' Tracy filled in, 'when Thompson asked if someone would show him the sights — '

'Right. I said we'd be happy to.'

'Actually you said *I'd* be happy to.'

'Well, I do have appointments. Besides, it's only for this afternoon; and, anyway, he specifically asked if you'd go with him.'

Tracy didn't know how to react. On the one hand it was flattering that he wanted her company; but on the other, this smacked of another ploy to get what he wanted. She felt her jaw tighten and her lips draw into a thin line. How she'd love to thwart him just to let him know he couldn't always win.

But Bill was waiting for her answer

and, of course, she had no good reason to deny his request. Until Titan Industries actually bought the hotel and tossed her out on her ear, she was employed to do what she was told. 'Of course I will. When and where?'

'I believe he's waiting in the lobby right now.'

Tracy sighed and rose from the chair. 'Consider me gone.'

Greg got up from his seat in the lobby the moment she came in and walked toward her. 'I want you to know how much I appreciate your acting as my tour guide today.' His smile seemed genuine, but Tracy felt there was a hint of humor behind his words.

'You and I both know,' she said, 'that you could do your sightseeing on your own. I suspect you don't like to take 'no' for an answer and that you're still trying to talk me into going to Fiji. Am I right?'

He grinned. 'Okay, you're right. I just want to know you better. Is that a crime?'

'So you don't really want to see any of the sights on Oahu?'

'Oh, I do.' He took her hand in his and once more his touch made a mockery of her hopes of keeping him out of her life.

She sighed. 'Okay, you've got yourself a guide for the afternoon. Where to?'

He put a hand under her elbow and led her toward the door. 'There are two things I've been told I must see: the Pearl Harbor Memorial and Punch Bowl.'

They drove in his rented convertible and Tracy told him what she knew about those sights. She'd only recently seen them herself, so some of the information was fresh in her mind. By the time she finished her recitation, they'd reached Punch Bowl, the crater of an extinct volcano now filled, not with lava, but with thousands of white crosses.

Greg stood beside her at the rim and gazed for a long time at the sight. The sky was cobalt blue, the grass bright green, the crosses glittering white in the sun. Here and there, flowers placed at crosses provided a few colorful accents. 'I had no idea,' Greg said, obviously moved by the sight.

They walked all around, read some of the names on the memorial and didn't speak again until she suggested they leave if they wanted to see Pearl Harbor before dark.

'It's getting too late and anyway, I've seen pictures of it. I'm not in the mood for looking down at the *Arizona* and realizing how many more men died too young. Let's find a restaurant and have an early dinner.'

Tracy directed him to an open-air buffet restaurant, and after making their selections from trays of fresh fruit, salads, breads and desserts, they found a table under a wide yellow umbrella and sat down.

'It makes you think, doesn't it?' he said finally.

'Think about what death?'

'Not just death, but the death of

young men. If I'd been born a lot earlier, I might have fought in that war, be under one of those crosses right now, perhaps never married, or even in love, my life cut short before it began.'

Tracy took a sip of her iced tea. 'It is sad, isn't it? But somebody had to stop Hitler and Hirohito.'

'I lived in San Francisco during the late sixties,' he said. 'I was only a kid, but the place was a hotbed of protest against our involvement in Vietnam. I remember seeing a poster that read, 'What if They Gave a War and Nobody Came?'' He paused. 'But we never learn.'

She mulled over his comments. They were similar to her own thoughts about war, and gave her another feeling of kinship with him. And yet, life wasn't that simple. 'How can countries not go to war when dictators and terrorists want to exterminate everyone who isn't like them? Don't we have an obligation to try to protect innocent people?'

He reached across the table and

squeezed her hand. 'Of course we do. As travel and other forms of communication grow, maybe we'll all become so interconnected we'll work together instead of fighting among ourselves.'

'That's one of the things I love about Hawaii,' Tracy said. 'There are so many different people here — Native Hawaiians, Europeans, Japanese, Chinese, Filipinos, Africans — and they all get along together. At least,' she said after a pause, 'they seem to. I haven't seen the racism that spoils some places on the mainland.'

He smiled and raised his glass. 'Here's to that.'

She clinked her glass to his and finished her meal.

He pushed his plate aside. 'I have an idea — let's go dancing.'

'I'm afraid I can't do that. I have duties, you know.'

'But it will get dark soon. Don't you get nights off? What kind of hours do you keep?'

'Hotels are open twenty-four hours a

day, seven days a week. Since I took this afternoon off, I need to check in with Bill to see if he needs me.' That was the truth, and she also felt that continuing to spend time with him undermined her vow not to get involved.

He shrugged. 'I guess if you must, you must. Thanks for this afternoon anyway.'

They drove back to the hotel and Tracy left him in the lobby. But, as she headed for her office, she could think of nothing but his request that they go dancing. The very thought of being in his arms, swaying to soft music, threatened to break rules about him she had yet to make up.

5

But Bill didn't need her services anymore that day; and, rather than retire to her room for the rest of the evening, Tracy changed into a swimsuit, grabbed her snorkeling gear and headed for the beach. There was still enough daylight, she decided, for a quick swim. She crossed the road and walked the twenty yards over the still-hot sand to the lava rocks that covered this part of the beach and extended for a distance into the water. Finding some smooth sand nearby, she spread out her striped towel and removed her sandals, then tied her hair into a ponytail with a length of scarlet ribbon from her tote bag. Lastly, she put on her swim fins.

Walking carefully to avoid stepping on the wide black webs of the fins, she entered the water, enjoying its coolness on her feet and legs. Wading forward, she stooped down and splashed water on her arms and then rinsed off her mask before slipping it over her head and adjusting the snorkel tube. Then she ducked under the water and swam off toward the rocks.

Blue and yellow striped tropical fish met her gaze, and nearly transparent needlefish swam close to the surface, always managing to stay out of her way. After swimming completely around the rock that jutted into the water, she took a deep breath and dove down to investigate the coral near the ocean floor. After several seconds, she bobbed back to the surface, blowing the water out of the tube as she came up. And almost collided with another swimmer.

Greg. He wasn't wearing a snorkeling mask and he grinned as if extremely proud of himself for having found her. 'So we meet again. I see you finished up your assistant manager duties in record time.'

Treading water, she pulled the breathing tube out of her mouth. 'I wasn't deliberately avoiding you, if that's what you're hinting.' But of course she was and the thought made her even more nervous. She said the first thing that came into her mind. 'What are you doing here?'

'Swimming. I was under the distinct impression that the state of Hawaii encourages people to swim in their ocean.' He continued to smile at her. 'I like it.'

'I'll send a bulletin to the Hawaii Visitors Bureau.'

'But no brass bands, please.'

She liked his friendly banter, but turned her head and glanced around for a moment. 'It's a huge ocean and this is a very wide beach. I can't believe you showed up at my side by accident.'

'Of course not. I saw you leaving the hotel, so I threw on my swim trunks and came after you.' He paused, used one hand to wipe saltwater from around his mouth. 'I sort of hoped you'd be pleased that I singled you out. Believe me, I passed a lot of bikini-clad beauties on my way to your rocks.'

He was right; the gorgeous women on Hawaiian beaches could easily outshine the cast of *Baywatch*. She smiled. 'Thanks for the compliment, but I've been snorkeling and you don't seem exactly dressed for the occasion.'

'No problem,' he said. 'I've snorkeled without fins or mask before.' With that, he dove under the water and she saw his long lean body glide effortlessly toward the rocks.

She put the tube back into her mouth and followed him, noticing with awe how long he could remain submerged before he had to come to the surface for air.

On their next dive, he pointed out a hole in the rock and Tracy could see an eel hiding in it. She backed away and headed for the surface again. She didn't like eels and some of them could be dangerous.

Greg's head bobbed up nearby, water cascading from his shiny dark hair. He shook his head, making his hair flip back from his forehead and sending drops of water into the balmy air. He looked totally at ease and Tracy felt that same stirring in her body that she'd felt before. She turned and swam back to shore, fairly certain he'd follow her there, too.

Once on the beach, she pulled off her mask and fins, walked to her towel and sat down, gesturing for him to do the same. It put him uncomfortably close to her, but she couldn't very well let him sit in the sand. Suddenly aware of his looking at her body in her high-cut swimsuit, she turned over on her stomach. 'So where did you snorkel before now?'

'Australia, when my dad was stationed there for a couple of years. The beaches are wonderful.' He paused. 'Most of the ladies go topless there, you know.'

'So I've heard.' She searched for a less intimate topic of conversation. 'What do you do in Los Angeles when you're not scouting out properties for your company to buy?'

'I swim there too, in Malibu.' He turned over onto his stomach, his tanned, very muscular arm grazing Tracy's. 'And go to the theater and pursue my hobbies.'

'What are your hobbies?'

'Believe it or not, I play bridge. My parents liked the game and I think they taught my brother and me so they'd have someone to practice with.'

Tracy closed her eyes in thought. 'My folks played cards, too. People of their generation did that sort of thing; but hardly anyone does now. I'm surprised that you can find partners.'

'I understand Bill Gates likes bridge, but, unfortunately, I don't move in his circles.'

'Nowadays people watch fifty channels of television or go to a gym.'

'Well, I do that too,' Greg admitted. 'The gym, that is. It's hard to get enough exercise without it.' He laughed lightly. 'And then I park in the closest place to the building and spend twenty minutes walking on the treadmill.'

Once more she liked the way he could laugh at himself, and it was easy to see that he got plenty of exercise. He seemed deliciously fit, with muscular shoulders and a firm midriff. 'But no television?'

'A little.' He paused. 'When I'm in town for a decent stretch of time I work for the Heritage Preservation Society.'

'You moonlight?' Tracy asked. She turned to look into his face, discovering it was only inches away from hers, making her feel strangely vulnerable.

'No, they don't pay me. I donate my time.'

'Doing what?' She was determined to keep the conversation on an impersonal level.

'It's a nonprofit group, funded by foundation grants and wealthy individuals who try to save historic structures from the wrecking ball.' He sighed. 'Well, I guess they don't use a wrecking ball anymore, they *implode* them.'

'What kind of historic places?'

'Churches, opera houses, Colonial or Victorian buildings.'

'How do you help save them?'

'I research their history, what makes them worth saving. Then I do public relations work to create public awareness and raise money to buy or restore them.' His voice turned serious and he raised himself on one elbow. 'It's really a shame, you know. Americans go to Europe to see those lovely old buildings, and here at home, we tear them down and put up something modern.'

Tracy shrugged. 'But who needs a bunch of old buildings that no one uses anymore?'

'Oh, they're used.' He turned and sat, bringing his knees up and wrapping his arms around them. 'I helped save a wonderful old Victorian mansion in San Francisco, and turn it into law offices. Even the inside remained almost the way it used to be, with high, sculptured ceilings and paneled walls.'

'Well,' Tracy said, 'I learned something new.' She turned over and sat up, brushed sand from her arms and legs. 'But now I think it's time I got back to the hotel.'

'I'll walk with you.'

The setting sun turned the ocean waves into silver ribbons. She saw it in her peripheral vision, beyond Greg, who folded her towel. Finished with that, his hand caught hers and he cupped her elbow lightly so she could slip into her sandals again. Then he steered her back across the road and through the darkening hotel garden. The air was filled with the fragrance of jasmine and the sound of water tumbling over rocks in the koi pond.

He led her off the path, deeper into the deserted garden, where night began to gather in long, dusky shadows. Why was she letting him do this? Why didn't she pull her hand away, go back into the hotel? Tracy couldn't think of an answer.

At an outcropping of lava rock, he

stopped, and finding a niche, moved into its protective shelter, bringing her with him. Still she seemed unable to protest. He held her close, tilted her head back. He lowered his so that his lips could brush against her temple, the bridge of her nose, her cheeks. One hand came across to rest against her bare back, his strong fingers pressing her closer.

She felt herself melting into his body, powerless to escape the mood he'd created. The swim fins and mask dropped from hands grown suddenly weak. When he kissed her, she put her arms around his waist, felt strong muscles under the flesh. She opened her lips under his and his tongue slipped inside for an instant. Ages passed before he broke the kiss.

She heard his soft whisper against her mouth. 'Come with me to Fiji.'

His words brought her back to reality. Another moment like that and there'd be no need to go to Fiji for a romantic liaison. She pushed herself from him at last. 'No, I can't.'

'You can if you want to.' He reached for her again.

Her whole body tingled with sensation. How could she feel so tempted, when deep inside she knew that the man and the night and the magic he was creating out of it had to be so wrong for her? In a week or two he'd be gone, and when — if, she corrected herself — the hotel became the property of Titan Industries, he wouldn't give a second thought to replacing her. Only last night, he had accused Paul of being a fool. What, then, did that make her?

'Let me go, Greg, please.' She turned away from him and ran across the garden until she reached the safety, the emptiness, of her room.

6

Sitting in the lobby of the Island Sands Hotel the next day, Tracy sipped her lemonade and looked across at Madeline, noticing the frown lines on her face.

'I might as well be frank about it,' Madeline was saying, 'my father took out several loans over the years and never told me.'

Tracy tried to get comfortable on the lumpy settee. She had left the Ocean Breeze and walked down Matau'u Road that morning for two reasons: to eliminate the chance of running into Greg Thompson, and to congratulate Madeline on her forthcoming marriage to Bill Griffin.

'I knew the hotel wasn't generating much extra cash,' Madeline continued, 'but I believed him when he said he had enough money put by. I think he hoped

I'd meet someone and get married instead of staying here to run this old place. Now, ironically, I'm doing both, marrying Bill *and* staying in Hawaii.'

In a sense, Tracy envied Madeline the freedom to make decisions. Yet, as she had told Greg, she had no desire to own a hotel. True, she had been fascinated by them ever since her first year of college, when she had taken a part-time job at the Lakeside, one of the North Shore's most exclusive hotels, owned by Matthew Westphal. The activity and excitement generated by the constant swirl of people in and out of the fabulous complex had convinced her that she'd enjoy a career that kept her in those surroundings.

But to own? No. Even the smallest hotel — and it would be outside the realm of reality to consider anything larger than an inn or a bed-and-breakfast — could quickly become an all-consuming enterprise. She had resolved early never to sacrifice her personal life, such as it was, for a business that could take all her waking hours just to keep solvent.

'I'm so pleased for both of you,' Tracy said.

'Thanks. We'd been making plans for some time. And now, with Bill's inheritance, we'll be able to pay off those loans, and do some of the remodeling we've talked about for the past year. These old ceiling fans, for instance.' She glanced at the one overhead. 'All they do is move the warm air around. We'll have to put in air conditioning to keep pace with the other, more modern hotels.'

'You will keep the fans, I hope,' Tracy said. 'They're so reminiscent of the past.'

'Of course we'll keep them,' Madeline said. 'We're the second oldest hotel in the area, and famous for our atmosphere, if nothing else. I'd remove them only at danger to my life.' She laughed. 'Also, we'll remodel the grand staircase to the second floor. And of course we're installing more elevators, too. The floors need replacing, and I want new carpeting and wallpaper everywhere.'

'Sounds like a long list.'

'In the year since my father died, I've had time to put a lot of things on it. The trouble is, people may like the outside to look like a vintage Polynesian hotel, but they expect the inside of their rooms to be strictly up-to-date. Bathrooms have to be shiny and modern, with hair dryers, coffee machines, telephones. I just hope my plans aren't too grand for Bill's windfall.'

Tracy finished her lemonade and set the glass on the low table. She agreed wholeheartedly. The way Bill had spoken yesterday, Tracy had assumed there would be enough money, but now that she heard her friend's plans, she wasn't so sure. Her heart went out to Madeline. Perhaps it would be years before she and Bill could restore the marvelous old place back to its former elegance.

Madeline stood up and smoothed her

long flowered blue dress. 'Let me give you that tour I promised,' she said, 'and you can see for yourself what I'm planning.'

Before she could move away, however, the receptionist, a young Polynesian girl, hurried up to her. 'Excuse me, Miss Hoff. You have a telephone call.' Madeline nodded and followed her to the desk in the lobby.

The fragrance of plumeria wafted in through the open lobby doors. While she waited, Tracy admired the brilliant red anthuriums in a bowl in the center of the table and fingered the neatly arranged magazines. At least *they* were up-to-date.

At that moment, the scream of an air-raid siren rent the air.

Tracy jumped up, her heart pounding. The wailing went on and on, and she visualized a scene from an old war movie, with enemy aircraft flying overhead, coming to drop bombs.

As abruptly as it began, the siren stopped. When Madeline returned a moment later, Tracy grabbed her arm. 'What was that?'

Madeline's voice was tinged with alarm and her frown had increased. 'That was a tsunami warning. Bill,' she added, 'was on the phone just now to tell me. Alaska had an earthquake and Hawaii is on a tsunami alert.'

Tracy felt her breath catch. 'A tsunami?'

'Tidal wave,' Madeline explained, her voice low and urgent. 'Even a distant earthquake can cause tidal waves through the entire Pacific. They think we may be in for trouble.'

Tracy looked around quickly at the rattan chairs and tables arranged around the lobby. Her imagination pictured a huge wall of water crashing down on the hotel, carrying everything off, drowning everyone.

'It could be a false alarm,' Madeline went on in a calmer voice, as if suddenly realizing she had communicated her own fears to Tracy. 'It's happened before. The authorities get excited, chase people off the beaches, and then nothing.' She reached out and touched Tracy's arm. 'That's probably what will happen again this time — nothing.'

Tracy wasn't fooled by Madeline's bravado. 'Do you really think so?'

'No,' the other woman admitted. 'It scares me just to think of it. It doesn't seem to matter how long I've lived here, and the false tidal wave alerts I've been through. I just remember reading about the times when people were killed and I wonder, is this the one?'

'I don't suppose I'll ever get used to it either.' Tracy's gaze shifted toward the screened door that led onto the broad veranda. 'I should get back to the Ocean Breeze and see if Bill needs my help.'

'Of course. And I'd better get busy here and start emergency procedures,' Madeline said. 'At least, your hotel is across the street from the ocean. Here, we're right on the beach.'

They crossed the lobby to the front

desk where someone had turned on a small radio, and they heard the voice of an announcer repeating the tsunami warning.

' — Local police are clearing all beaches and certain buildings and urging residents to move to higher ground. Stay tuned to this station for further information as soon as it becomes available.'

★ ★ ★

Less than an hour later, Tracy rushed down the first floor corridor of the west wing of the Ocean Breeze, knocking on doors to alert the guests that the switchboard operator had not been able to reach. In the all-too-few minutes she'd had to talk to Bill, who was barking orders to three other people at the same time, he had informed her that the first item on the emergency procedures list was to send everyone to the roof for safety.

She had covered most of the rooms

on the first floor when she arrived at number 123. To her surprise the door opened almost at once to reveal Greg Thompson, his gleaming, tanned torso slashed midway with the white of a hotel towel, his face still wet under tousled dripping hair.

He's supposed to be in Fiji, Tracy thought, dismayed. She watched a bead of water roll in slow motion down his cheek and over his jaw. Not a sound passed his lips, no 'how are you?' or 'what brings you to my door?' or 'by the way, I enjoyed that kiss last night!' Even a simple 'hello' would have done quite nicely under the circumstances.

'You didn't go to Fiji.' She regretted her own words as soon as they were spoken. She hadn't even said 'hello' herself. Talk about congenial.

'I decided to wait another day.' He shrugged. 'Just in case.' His body language told her he didn't really expect her to run off with him for the day.

'It seems you should have,' she said, ignoring the personal implications. 'There's been a tsunami alert.'

'Tsunami?' He raked his wet hair with his fingers. Already it was beginning to curl at the ends. 'What's being done to warn people?'

'Radio and television, of course,' Tracy said, 'and here in the hotel we're trying to encourage everyone to go up to the roof.'

He looked both ways down the long corridor, where a double row of doors — twenty-two in all — faced each other. 'I'll need a minute to get dressed, then I'll give you a hand.'

'You don't have to volunteer yourself,' Tracy told him.

But he had already disappeared into the bedroom, only to emerge within minutes wearing pale blue slacks, and pulling a polo shirt over his head.

'Right,' Tracy said with a wry laugh, noting once again how skilled he was at getting his way. However, in this instance, she didn't mind. 'Why don't you take the even numbers and I'll take the odd?'

His long fingers closed around hers and he gave her hand a squeeze before crossing the corridor and knocking on number 124. With her back to him, it was easier to shut him out of her thoughts and concentrate on the potential danger coming at them from across the ocean, a danger she had never experienced and could only imagine. As she proceeded, his voice occasionally drifted across the corridor and her awareness of him would come rushing in again, a reminder that the complex sensations he had aroused in her were not likely to be put to rest anytime soon.

Then at room 135, an elderly Japanese woman in a kimono, carrying an ebony cane, opened the door. As frail-looking as a butterfly, she barely reached Tracy's shoulder, and throughout the explanation of why she must leave her room, she continuously shook her head.

Terrific, Tracy thought. *I can't speak Japanese. How am I going to get her to understand me?* She had just started a pantomime, along with a louder version of her instructions, when Greg came up behind her.

'Having trouble?' he asked.

'Yes, this woman apparently doesn't understand English. We have several Japanese-speaking employees, but I haven't the faintest idea where to find any of them now.'

'Why don't you let me try?' Greg stepped in front of her, bowed low to the tiny old woman and spoke in rapid Japanese. Tracy's eyes widened.

The woman replied, and pointed to her cane, and again Greg spoke in her language. Finally, he turned back to Tracy.

'Her name is Mrs. Kanaya and she's very worried, because she needs a cane to walk and tries to avoid elevators. That's why her room is down here on the first floor. I told her I would help her up to the roof. You go ahead and finish here and I'll meet you on the second floor.'

Tracy smiled her gratitude as Greg offered his arm to Mrs. Kanaya, who accepted it with a look of obvious relief. Together they started slowly down the corridor toward the bank of elevators. What a picture in contrasts, Tracy thought, hardly able to tear her eyes away from them. But then the immediacy of the situation returned and again she forced Greg Thompson to the back of her mind and moved on to the next room.

She had reached the third floor before Greg appeared again, striding quickly down the hall.

'Sorry to be so late joining you,' he said. 'When I got upstairs, I found that they were moving chairs from the coffee shop up to the roof, so I helped unload them. Bill was there and seems to want a first-aid station set up too, just in case. I volunteered to tell you.'

'Thanks.' Tracy lingered near him for

a moment. 'We're almost through here anyway.'

'Why don't you let me finish this, then,' Greg asked, 'and you do your first-aid thing? I'll join you there later.'

'You really don't have to get involved in this,' she reminded him. 'You're a guest — '

'I hope I'm a little more than that,' he said. 'And I was glad to do it. I'd enjoy doing anything with you.'

As much to clear her thoughts of the man as to remain on schedule, she agreed and hurried along the corridor to the elevators. She could feel his gaze following her, but the sense of urgency that had dominated the past two hours claimed her again and she pushed Greg Thompson from the forefront of her attention. She told herself that he meant nothing to her, nothing at all.

She descended to the ground floor again, found the first-aid supplies in the linen room, then took the elevator to the roof. The place resembled a giant cocktail party with lots of activity and the constant hum of voices. She discovered that aside from the hotel guests, nearby residents who lived in the small houses behind Matau'u Road had gathered here as well. Apparently, they'd used this refuge before during tidal wave alerts.

She looked down into the street. Police cars still patrolled, their loud-speakers announcing every few seconds that all people must leave the beaches and go to higher ground. There she saw people on foot, and vehicles of every description driving toward the hills.

A food bar had been set up in one corner of the roof, and the smell of pineapple, grilled sandwiches and fresh-brewed coffee reminded Tracy that somehow it had become late afternoon without her knowing it. Part of the strange feeling in her middle must be the result of having had no lunch. Ignoring it, she descended once more and found Bill in the deserted lobby.

'I've set up the first-aid station,' she

told him. 'Is there anything else I can do?'

'No, we seem to have done everything we can. The rest is up to Mother Nature.'

Mother Nature. Ever since the *El Niño* storms of '98, she'd been wary of that lady. Like millions of people all over the world, Tracy had learned what destructive forces the elements could unleash. A shiver ran up her spine.

7

Tracy shuddered at the thought of the possible results of a huge tidal wave. Then she realized Bill was still staring at her.

As if he'd noticed the concern in her face, he said, 'I hope I haven't alarmed you too much. After all, the Pacific Ocean is huge. By the time a tidal wave from Alaska gets all the way out to us, it may very well diminish considerably in force. I wouldn't be surprised if our worst problem will be putting everything back where it belongs again.'

Tracy smiled at him, but for some reason she didn't feel nearly so confident. Why? After all, Bill had lived in Hawaii for many years; she, on the other hand, was a newcomer. She'd learned a lot in three months, but she knew nothing about earthquakes and tidal waves.

But she shrugged and tried to appear as optimistic as he was. 'How will we know when the danger is over?'

'There'll be an all-clear whistle — like the one that started this — that will blast your eardrums,' he said. 'Frankly, I'm expecting it any minute. It's been a long time since the first alert, and that wave, if it's coming, should have been here by now. I think we can relax.'

'Then I'll go back up and get something to eat,' she said. 'I'm starved.'

Five minutes later, Tracy looked for a place to sit down. Although every extra chair had been moved to the roof, she found them all occupied and she perched on the concrete ledge, setting her tuna salad sandwich, bag of potato chips and cup of coffee beside her.

'Here you are.' Greg appeared at her side.

At the sight of his clean, handsome profile, Tracy's weariness seemed to melt away. She smiled.

'I was going to invite you to have dinner with me, but I see you've beaten me to it.'

'You can get a sandwich over there.' Tracy indicated a long white cloth-covered table protected by a striped green awning.

'Actually, I'm not very hungry,' he said, leaning against the concrete ledge so that his body almost touched her knee. 'I'd rather just look at you.'

Her face warmed at his words. 'Thanks for all your help today,' she said, ignoring the flirtatiousness of his last remark. 'Especially with Mrs. Kanaya.'

'My pleasure.'

'It was uncanny, my needing someone to speak Japanese' — she gave a little laugh — 'and there you were.'

He grinned and moved closer to her. 'I'm glad you need me. That must mean we're making progress.'

She shifted her position on the wall, crossing and uncrossing her legs. She wondered if he noticed that, when she settled again, the space between them had widened by several inches. If he was disappointed, he hid it well.

'Where did you learn Japanese?' she asked.

'In Japan. I spent eight years there when I was a child.'

'You lived in Japan?'

'Yes. My father worked for the State Department.'

She tried to picture him as a child, tall for his age and probably gangly, wearing Japanese clothes. 'Did you enjoy it?'

'Of course. I'd lived in almost every part of the world by the time I was eighteen. Fortunately, I never had a problem adjusting to different cultures. As for languages, I was even luckier. I picked them up pretty easily.'

'Languages?' Tracy said. 'Plural? How many do you speak?'

'Five, counting English. But of the foreign languages, I'm most fluent in Japanese.'

'You must have had an interesting childhood.'

'Hmmm,' he agreed, nodding. 'It was better than some, I suppose, but not entirely without growing pains. There were plenty of those along the way.' He looked into her eyes. 'How about you?'

'Me?' She shrugged. 'I had a very conventional childhood. Lived in one place — Chicago — all my life. I went to public school, became a Girl Scout, learned to swim and sail and ice skate on the lake. Had a few childhood traumas, nothing serious.' *Those came later*, she almost said, but the last thing she needed was to rehash those last few months with Paul.

She came down off the ledge and looked out over the roof railings at the silent sea. 'Pretty dull stuff.'

He shook his head. 'Not if you were there.'

She wished he wouldn't do that, say those kinds of things. 'It wasn't very exotic. While you were learning five languages, I was making do with one.' She smiled and glanced at him out of the corner of her eye. 'Two, if you really want to stretch it I studied French for three years, but never managed to speak like a native.'

'Who cares about the French anyway?' He caught her gaze and grinned.

'You managed it, though — to speak like a native, I mean.'

'I have Japanese friends in Los Angeles. I owe my fluency to them. But my accent leaves a lot to be desired.'

In spite of every protective barrier Tracy had tried to erect, she found herself wondering if any of these very close friends were women. Or, more to the point, one woman. She began to get a mental image of a petite, delicate Asian beauty waiting for Greg in Los Angeles.

'Do you like Japanese food?'

'What?' His sudden question shattered the image. 'Oh, yes. Anyway, I think so, the little I've had of it. And that was only the usual dishes, sukiyaki, tempura, chicken. Most of it tasted suspiciously western, even to me.' She grinned.

'Someday,' he said, tilting her chin up, 'I'm going to cook an authentic Japanese meal for you. I may not be the best cook,' he added hastily, 'but I promise you'll have no trouble distinguishing east from west.'

Someday. How perfectly vague, and rightfully so, she thought, turning her head away. That someday was not likely to come soon. Such a day wasn't likely to come at all. She'd traveled six thousand miles to get away from her failed romance with Paul and she couldn't let herself become interested in a man she'd never see again.

He sensed her mood at once. 'I've said something wrong. Whatever it was, I take it back.'

Doubts plagued her, stronger than ever. He would return to Los Angeles in time, and she was determined not to let that event disrupt her life. 'It's nothing important.'

'It is to me,' he said. He took her free hand in his and touched it lightly to his lips. 'I've enjoyed being with you today.

And yesterday, and last night — '

'Forget last night,' she said, almost too sharply, and then instantly regretted using that tone of voice with him. But she had to make him understand. She pulled her hand away.

'Did Bill tell you he was leaving the hotel in two weeks?'

Greg nodded.

'And did he tell you he's recommending me for manager?'

'He mentioned it.'

'Even with Bill's recommendation, there are no guarantees; but if your company buys the hotel, that opportunity will vanish.'

'You don't know that for a fact, and I certainly don't.' He raised one hand as if to touch her again, then dropped it to his side.

'What I know,' she said, 'is how few women managers there are in this business. I read a magazine story that profiled the managers of eight large American hotels. Without exception, they were all men.'

'All right, so I admit that life can sometimes be unfair. But that kind of attitude is changing all the time.'

'Who manages La Casa Grande in Mexico?' she asked simply.

He held up his hands, defeated.

'You see, it isn't changing fast enough.'

'Would it help if I steered Titan away from buying the Ocean Breeze? There's more than enough to keep them interested out here without that.'

Tracy's temper flared momentarily. 'I don't want any favors from you.'

In the pause that followed, she realized she could barely see his expression, for the sky had darkened considerably. The few dim lights on the roof did little to pierce the growing gloom; and in the flickering of their beams, the firm outline of Greg's jaw took on added strength.

But there was more than strength about this man. His courtesy and gentleness toward Mrs. Kanaya had impressed her, and now he had offered to lead Titan away from the purchase of the hotel for her sake. In addition, she could not deny the electricity that had flowed between them from the very first moment she had caught him looking at her from the railing of the cruise ship. Nevertheless, no matter how difficult it would be to resist, she would not permit anything to come of it.

'I'm sorry,' she said, 'but I must leave. I have something important to check on,' and she turned from him and began to walk away.

He caught her hand. 'I hope you aren't going back downstairs. It's just as important for the staff to remain out of harm's way as it is for the guests, you know.'

'I won't be long,' she told him. 'I've been having a nagging suspicion that I forgot to put the accounts book back in the safe last night, and today I've been too busy to go back and look.'

His expression showed concern and he didn't release her hand. 'Better the accounts book drowns than you.'

'Really,' she said, pulling her hand away, 'you make it sound as if I'm taking my life in my hands. Nothing will happen to me. Bill says these alerts come up all the time and there's never a tsunami.'

'Maybe Bill doesn't know about them.'

His tone was solemn and Tracy felt her forehead begin to tighten into a frown. 'What do you mean?'

'I lived in Japan, remember? The word tsunami is Japanese and we had quite a few alerts — which people took very seriously. In 1960 there was a 6.8 earthquake that caused a devastating tsunami wave in Japan. People were killed.' He paused. 'It happened before I was born, but they still talked about it years later.'

Surely, Tracy thought, that couldn't happen again. After all, he'd been a child when he lived in Japan and stories of killer tidal waves had scared him, made an impression on his young mind. 'Well, perhaps they didn't have warning systems in Japan way back then.'

'People have been killed by tsunami waves in Hawaii too, Tracy. Over 150 in 1946 and several as recently as 1975. Look it up.'

'How did you become such an expert on the subject?'

'As I said, living in Japan made me aware of tsunamis in the first place, but I heard of so many after that, they sort of stuck in my mind. I'm sure you remember the one in Papua, New Guinea, a year or so ago. That earthquake occurred only twelve miles off the coast and a twenty-three-foot tsunami wave struck land minutes later, demolishing an entire village. There was no time for warnings and more than 2,000 people were killed.'

Tracy did remember reading about that; but she had been living in Chicago then and New Guinea seemed too remote to mean much of anything to her, although she'd been shocked at the mere thought of so many deaths. Still, determined not to let his story scare her, she moved to the elevators and pressed the signal button.

Suddenly the elevator doors swished open in front of her, and she had to make a decision. She stepped inside, turned and gave him a forced smile. 'I'll be right back. Scout's honor.'

She pushed the down button, and let it take her back to the lobby floor, all the while telling herself Greg's fears were exaggerated. Besides, she'd hurry.

When the doors opened on the ground floor, she saw that the corridor was deserted, with only lights from emergency lamps providing a dim glow. She walked through the lobby, slipped behind the front desk, and went into her office. The hotel checkbook and a ledger lay open on her desk, her discarded pencil resting in the fold. She picked them up quickly, glad that she had remembered. Going into Bill's office, she dialed the combination to the safe, which held important office records and daily receipts. After reclosing the heavy metal door, she returned to the lobby.

The utter silence arrested her. It gave everything an eerie, surreal quality, reminding Tracy of a scene from a science fiction movie where, suddenly, everyone disappears. The emptiness was strangely fascinating and, as her eyes roamed over the vacant couches and chairs — which, at this time of evening were usually occupied by guests — she shivered.

Then her attention turned to the front doors, and she found herself drawn toward the entrance that faced Matau'u Road. Her curiosity getting the best of her, she stepped out onto the porch and into the inky shadows cast by a nearly full moon.

Descending the four steps that led from the porch to the flagstone path that paralleled the wide circular drive, she continued walking toward the street, past tiki plants, small bamboo and banana trees, and a tiny rock-lined waterfall, and finally to the broad sidewalk that edged Matau'u Road. Visible to passersby because of its sloping construction, the entry garden was Tracy's favorite and added to the charming natural look of the hotel grounds.

Feeling guilty for being there instead of upstairs, she promised herself again that she wouldn't stay long. She walked to the street. It was deserted, as was the beach on the other side. The water, to her view, seemed no different than it was on any other evening. Tiny whitecaps topped the gentle waves, and the sound of them lapping at the shore was the same lullaby that helped her fall asleep at night. But the people were gone. Many were on the roof of the Ocean Breeze; others, dutifully, had fled to higher ground.

Not once in the time she'd been in the Islands had she ever seen the beach so completely deserted. Even late at night, or in the first light of dawn, someone was always there: usually surfers, who seemingly needed little light to mount their boards, paddle out to the incoming waves and then ride them gracefully back to shore.

Now, in the distance, she saw that dozens of boats dotted the water. Bobbing on the darkening blue of the ocean, they reminded Tracy that they, too, were waiting for the tidal wave and had put out to sea to prevent being dashed to pieces against the piers should the tsunami really come.

She turned and began to walk back toward the porch. The silence caught her attention. The lapping of waves had stopped, as if someone had turned off a faucet. Then she heard a whisper, faint at first, then louder and louder, until it grew into a strange sucking noise. Standing still, she looked toward the water — but it was gone. Where were the waves? Why did there seem to be nothing but sand as far as she could see? What had happened to the ocean?

Then she saw it. As if rooted to the spot, she couldn't move a muscle. Open-mouthed, she watched as a large wave rushed at the beach. It pounded across the sand, engulfed the plants that grew at its edge, surged into the street and across it, spilled over the sidewalk and raced toward the hotel. Toward her.

8

Too late, Tracy turned and fled to the hotel porch. She heard the roar of water behind her; then a wave crashed into her back and sent her sprawling onto the ground.

No, she screamed in her head.

The force of the water threw her onto the porch steps. She banged against them, feeling a stab of pain across the top of her head. As suddenly as she was thrown forward, she was dragged backward, back from the steps, back across the path. She grabbed for something, anything, to hold on to; but the fragile flower stalks that lined the path broke off in her hands. She felt herself being tossed like a rag doll. Her elbows and knees scraped across the flagstones. She was being pulled into the ocean.

She clutched at small shrubs as she

tumbled backward. She slammed into a tree and tried to put her arms around its slender trunk but it was no use. The pull of the tide was too strong. Water filled her eyes, her ears, her mouth. She couldn't breathe. She was going to drown.

Suddenly a voice yelled, 'Tracy!' and, almost at the same instant, she felt strong arms encircle her waist. She was being half-carried, half-dragged out of the water. Greg!

Choking and sputtering, she clutched him, and felt herself being pulled toward the lanai. Her feet hit the first step and then he dragged her upward. A second step, another, and they were standing at the top of the porch. A second wave slammed at them, and a foot of water flooded across the porch.

Tracy clung to Greg, while the wave flung a curtain of spray into the air around them, soaking their hair and faces. In spite of his tight hold on her, Tracy felt the water eddying back around her legs, pulling her off balance.

The wooden planks underfoot were slick and treacherous and she felt herself slipping and sliding, helpless to keep the wave from dragging her back into the ocean.

Greg released one arm from around her and grabbed one of the pillars that supported the lanai roof. His other arm tightened, holding her against him. Suddenly, Tracy could no longer feel the cold water, only the heat from Greg's body where the long length of him touched her. Another wave, smaller this time, rushed in, spilling over the steps below them.

They didn't move and Tracy held her breath. Greg turned slightly, looking down at the receding water.

'The worst is over, I think.' As if to punctuate his sentence, a fourth wave sent a mere inch of foam across the path, and then the usual rhythm of the ocean resumed.

She glanced at his face, and saw the look in his eyes change from anxiety to relief. She might have drowned — they both might have drowned. The tidal wave had come after all.

She pressed her cheek against his shirt, wishing he would go on holding her like this forever. She was safe.

'I've heard of having the ocean at your doorstep,' he said wryly, 'but this is ridiculous.' He laughed softly against her wet hair.

She continued to hold him. 'Thank you,' she said in a choked whisper. 'If you hadn't come along just then — '

He didn't loosen his hold on her. 'I was worried so I went to look for you. Good thing I did.'

She felt the last of the fear ease from her body.

Seconds turned into minutes and still they clung together. She could hear Greg's breathing, feel his heart beating in his chest, his hand moving across her back through the thin fabric of her dress.

'Tracy.' His voice rasped against her cheek. 'Do you feel it, too?' He pulled her into the shadows. She lifted her face and his mouth came down on hers, warm and eager, with a hard, urgent edge that drove every thought from her mind except the need to experience this moment.

When at last he broke the kiss, his voice was hoarse. 'Stay with me tonight.'

The words shocked her into reality. She backed away from him and glanced down at herself. She was soaking wet her dress was clinging to her body, and her knees and elbows were scraped and bleeding. She pushed her sodden hair from her face and looked up at him.

'Greg, don't.' She shook her head as if to deny the intensity of the feelings that had swept through her just moments ago. 'Don't even think such things.'

'Why not?'

'Because it's impossible.' Why couldn't he try to understand? How could he ever be a part of her life, or she of his? The tidal wave, and his rescuing her, hadn't changed anything.

'Does my being here only a few weeks bother you that much?'

Tracy moaned. 'You have a diabolical way of reading my mind. Of course it bothers me.'

'Don't let it.'

'Ha!'

'Listen, Tracy.' He took her elbow in his strong hand, pivoting so that the right side of his body leaned into her left. 'I'm vulnerable, too. I stand to risk and lose as much as you. But I'm willing to give it a chance.'

She believed him immediately on pure instinct. There was a sincerity and wholesomeness about Greg Thompson that attracted her as much as the sensual side of him. He wasn't immune to hurt, she realized. He had come away from an unsuccessful marriage that must have left its scars. That, however, did not lessen the problems.

She tried again. 'In spite of just now, in spite of last night,' she said quietly, 'I'd like to have it clear between us that I'm not interested in an affair. For a

115

number of reasons. Please don't take it personally.'

'I don't know how else to take it.' His dark eyes became thoughtful. 'We seem to think differently. I don't look at a woman and think, 'Shall I have an affair with this one or not? Will we fall in love or wind up hating each other?' Either there's chemistry between us, or there isn't. In our case, I think there is a very definite chemistry.' He touched the side of her face lightly. 'And you may take that as personally as you like.'

Tracy's throat tightened. 'Has it ever occurred to you that you might be mistaken?'

'No,' he said in a deep, caressing voice, 'and certainly I didn't misread you last night or just a few moments ago.'

Tracy had to admit that he hadn't, as she relived in exquisite detail the times when he had held her tightly, kissed her passionately. And she had wanted it, enjoyed it, every bit as much as he had.

'We both felt something,' he said

softly. 'Admit it.'

Admit it? What could he possibly know of her feelings, of the silent battle being fought inside her? But she didn't have to answer, because just then a shriek rent the air once more and she realized that the all-clear had sounded.

9

Tracy dashed inside the building and rushed to her room, pulling off her soggy clothes as soon as she'd closed the door. She dropped them in the bathroom, reached inside the shower and turned the hot water on full blast. When she was finally standing naked under the spray, she relaxed her tense muscles and lifted her head up, letting the water flow over her body.

For an instant, an image appeared in her mind: her naked body next to Greg's, his hands gently caressing her willing flesh. She stood up very straight. A *cold* shower was probably what she really needed.

She grabbed the soap and loofah and scrubbed herself, as if the ritual would eliminate even her erotic thoughts. Then she reached for the shampoo, washed her hair quickly and put her head directly under the water to rinse away everything, including the memory of Greg's touch.

She wanted to linger under the soothing stream, but duty beckoned again. Although it was growing late, she would be needed to help restore order to the hotel before she could call it a night.

As she towel-dried her hair, she realized with gratitude that the hotel had suffered no damage. She ought to know; she had been right there when the wave crashed over the porch. Succeeding waves hadn't reached that level so, at most, there would be only a wet outer lobby floor that would need mopping before the furniture could be brought back from where it had been stored. Of course, the front garden — where the waves had smashed into the plantings — would need attention; but, here in Hawaii, everything grew so fast that in three weeks she probably wouldn't be able to see any evidence of the event.

She ran a comb lightly through her damp hair, then checked her arms and legs for bruises. The scrapes were healing already, with no bleeding, and only two places — one on her upper arm, and one on her knee — required a small adhesive bandage. That done, she pulled on blue cotton pants and a white T-shirt and hurried out of her apartment.

The lobby was a beehive of activity: bellboys, maids and other employees worked at restoring order to the first floor. In addition to the usual soft Hawaiian music that came from hidden speakers throughout the lobby, she heard the hum of elevators, raised voices, even laughter, as people returned from their emergency shelter on the roof. Almost at once she spotted Bill, hauling chairs back to the coffee shop.

She joined him. 'What can I do?'

He looked up, smiling, delighted that the tidal wave had passed and they were safe again. 'Just undo what you did before,' he said. 'Everyone's being so helpful, we'll have it all finished in no time.'

Tracy went to the bank of elevators and waited until one descended with a full load of guests. They were chatting to one another, excited to be on hand for the tidal wave but a little disappointed that the actual event had been so mild. As she rose toward the roof, she wondered how happy those guests would have been if the worst had happened. Oh, they were safe enough — the building was concrete and steel, after all — but a flood of water could have carried away, or ruined, everything in their rooms.

Her thoughts were interrupted by the elevator doors opening at the roof level, where she saw restaurant employees dismantling the food station and carrying equipment to the service elevators. She gathered up the first-aid supplies, returned them to their boxes, and carried them back toward the elevator.

As the door opened, Greg stepped

out in front of her. He, too, had put on dry clothes and looked as impeccably groomed as ever. 'Tracy,' was all he said.

Involuntarily, she stepped back slightly. 'Oh. Greg.' At first, she couldn't think what to say to him, how to comment on their being together in front of the hotel when the tidal wave came. She didn't like thinking of that, remembering her monumental stupidity in having gone outside instead of back up to the hotel roof. Yet, she couldn't ignore his part in that episode.

'Thanks again for rescuing me. You probably saved my life.' She moved around him then, and stepped into the elevator, pressing the down button with her elbow.

He hurried inside with her. 'Let me help you with that.' He took the box of first-aid supplies from her arms.

She gave him a small smile and then looked straight ahead at the closed doors, feeling the elevator begin its descent. Why should she feel so uncomfortable with him now, when only a short time ago she'd been melting in his arms? But she knew why. It was because melting in the arms of a man who might be instrumental in destroying her career was not on her agenda. She had to remember that and not allow herself to be swayed by the chemistry between them.

Greg broke the awkward silence. 'About saving your life,' he said. 'Do you know the ancient belief that if you save someone's life, you're responsible for that person from then on?'

Tracy glanced over at him. 'Yes, I've heard that superstition.'

'Well, then, you sort of belong to me.' He grinned as if he'd just won a million-dollar lottery or been knighted by some king.

'I don't belong to anyone,' Tracy told him quietly. 'I hereby absolve you of any future responsibility for me.'

The elevator doors opened on the lobby floor, and Tracy stepped out and headed for the linen storage room with

Greg a step behind her.

'It's not as simple as that,' he was saying. 'You can't absolve me. The gods have decreed that by saving your life, I've taken on the role of your protector. Whether you like it or not,' he added jovially.

They had reached the linen storage room now and Tracy pushed open the door and stepped aside. 'Just set the box on the shelf,' she told Greg. Then she turned and started back toward her office. Once more he followed.

When she didn't respond to his last statement, he persisted. 'What do you think of that?'

She stopped and turned to face him, lowering her voice so that none of the many people crowding the lobby could hear her. 'I don't believe you've thought this through. How can you be my protector when I intend to stay right here in Hawaii and your job is in Los Angeles? As a matter of fact, aren't you supposed to be looking at property in Fiji right now?'

'All the more reason you need to come with me.' His grin widened.

She couldn't help laughing. 'You have an answer for everything, don't you?'

'One tries.'

She put her hands on her hips. 'One had better get used to the idea that I'm not your responsibility and, most especially, that I refuse to be part of your little scenario.'

'Curses. Foiled again.' He shook his head, sending his shock of dark hair across his forehead.

His humor was beguiling and Tracy regretted the need to steer clear of this man, lest she fall in love with him against her better judgment. She shrugged, turned, and walked away.

Greg didn't follow this time. 'So — ?' he asked.

'So, go to Fiji,' she said over her shoulder.

10

Tracy awoke with a start, one thought hammering in her brain: the Island Sands. Guilt drove her from her bed to shower and dress quickly. How could she have forgotten about her friend Madeline, about what the tsunami might have done to her hotel? The Ocean Breeze was across the street from the beach; yet the tidal wave had come crashing toward it, onto the porch, leaving a film of water on the lobby floor. What had it done to the Island Sands, which was right *on* the beach?

She ran from her room and hurried to the coffee shop for a stand-up breakfast of pineapple juice, coffee and a croissant, all the while glancing at her watch. Only six-thirty, thank goodness; there was time to get to the other hotel and back before her duties began.

With the coffee in a foam cup in her hand, she rushed to the manager's office to tell Bill Griffin where she was going. But he wasn't there. Perhaps he wasn't yet awake. But even as this thought crossed her mind, she dismissed it. If *she* was worried about Madeline, what about Bill, who was engaged to the woman, who was making plans to use his inheritance to upgrade her hotel?

Back in the lobby again, Tracy found the night receptionist behind the desk. 'Poppy,' she called, and the young woman jumped from her chair, pushing her dark hair away from her face as she came.

'Yes, Miss Barnes?'

'Have you seen Mr. Griffin this morning?'

'Yes. He said to tell you he's gone to the Island Sands.'

Tracy was relieved to know that he'd gone there, but it presented her with a dilemma. As assistant manager, she needed to stay in the hotel when the manager was away, even though she wanted desperately to offer her support — and possibly help — to her friend.

She felt the guilt return. She should have thought of this last night and gone straight over there instead of having gone to bed. Yet, the events of the day and evening, the tidal wave that almost claimed her as a victim, thoughts of Greg saving her life and her response to his kisses, and then the clean-up operation, had all devoured her attention, leaving her feeling drained and disconcerted. After all that, she was fortunate to remember her name, much less what might have happened a mile away.

But that was no excuse, she told herself. She *ought* to have thought of Madeline, of the danger to a hotel right on the beach when the tsunami struck. Her jaw felt tight and tears of frustration threatened to erupt. She forced herself to smile at Poppy; then she stepped behind the desk and headed back to her own office.

She set the cup of coffee down and picked up the phone. At least she could call Madeline and find out what had happened. But the number rang and rang and no one answered. Her anxiety increased. What was going on there?

A sound behind her made her turn quickly. Greg stood in her doorway. He wore a white shirt, blazer and slacks and looked wide awake in spite of the early hour.

'I've come to tell you I'm taking your advice and going to Fiji this morning.'

Still worrying about Madeline, she didn't answer, and he continued. 'I didn't really expect to find you up so early, but since you are, I can ask you again if you'd like to come with me.' He leaned against the doorjamb and grinned.

She cleared her throat. 'Even if I wanted to go with you, I couldn't. Bill's gone and I'm the manager here until he gets back.'

'He's gone?' Greg asked.

'To the Island Sands Hotel.' She gave

him a brief resumé of the situation: She told him that Bill and Madeline were engaged, that the Sands was right on the beach, and that Bill had undoubtedly gone there first thing this morning — or even late last night — to determine what damage the tidal wave might have caused.

'I see,' was all he said for a moment. 'So, in effect, you're stuck here.'

'Stuck is the operative word,' she admitted. She looked around her small office. All was neat and tidy and she really had no pressing duties to perform. Mainly, she was just on call in case something came up. 'Far from flying to Fiji, what I really want to do is go to the Island Sands myself. Madeline is my best friend. I want to help.'

'How do you know she needs help?'

'I tried to telephone but no one answers. It's a hotel,' she said, raising her voice, 'someone must answer the telephone at a hotel.' She felt her uneasiness increasing again, and picked up her coffee to take another swallow.

Greg glanced at his watch. 'It's early. Can't you just run over for a few minutes?'

'It's a mile away and I haven't got a car. Bill has no doubt taken the hotel car himself. Normally, I like walking there, but I can't spare the time now.'

'Then let me drive you.'

Tracy looked up at him and didn't answer for a moment. Then remembering, she said, 'Don't you have to catch a plane?'

'I'll take a later one.'

'No, you mustn't do that. I don't want to be responsible for you missing your flight and upsetting all your business plans.'

'I have no appointments that can't wait. I've learned already that no one in this part of the world does anything by the clock. I think they operate on their own kind of time — not Standard, not Daylight, but Island Time.'

She couldn't help smiling. She'd experienced that phenomenon herself her first week in Hawaii. Just *try* to get a delivery person to show up when you need one.

'Well, it's settled then,' he said. 'I'll drive you over and back and you can see for yourself what's happened.' He paused. 'To tell the truth, you've aroused my curiosity. I'd like to see the effects of the tsunami, if that's the problem.'

Still Tracy hesitated. Just where did her priorities lie: Should she stay here on the job, or find out how her friend was faring?

Greg seemed to sense her hesitation. 'Half an hour.'

★ ★ ★

Five minutes after telling Poppy where she was going, Tracy was rushing out the door with Greg. She gave him directions and he drove quickly, although not quickly enough to satisfy her. At last they climbed out of his rental car in front of the Island Sands. Dozens of cars and taxis crowded the entry and the street, and people were hustling out of the building, carrying suitcases, garment bags, or just armloads of belongings.

As she stepped onto the street, Tracy noticed that it was coated with a layer of wet sand, interspersed with pieces of tropical plants, soggy leaves, wilted flowers, and palm fronds. She plunged through the debris, feeling her sandals become soaked and gritty, heading for the double doors that stood open above the veranda. Greg followed, only a step behind.

Inside seemed little different from outside. In the lobby, the once beautiful parquet floors were covered with sand and muck, the wood visible only where suitcases had been dragged across it or people had walked through it on their way out. More people clogged the lobby, clustered at the front desk, or hurried down the grand staircase. Voices were raised to an angry pitch and telephones jangled.

Tracy headed for the desk, craning

her neck, trying to see if Madeline or Bill was behind the counter. Greg, being taller, had no trouble seeing the crowd.

'Griffin isn't there,' he told Tracy. 'I don't know what your friend Madeline looks like, but there are only three people behind the desk, two young men and a Hawaiian girl who looks all of seventeen.'

'Not Madeline,' Tracy said. 'Where could they be?' And then a terrible thought came to her. 'Are they — ?'

Greg seemed to read her mind again. 'Dead? No, don't even think it. Things are a mess, but I'm sure everyone's still alive.'

'How can you be certain? What if — ?'

'Well, for one thing,' Greg said, interrupting her, 'there'd be an ambulance outside.'

Tracy wasn't sure she believed him — after all, the ambulance could have come and gone already — but she clung to the hope that he was right.

She pushed through the crowd of people and started for the staircase, but Greg caught her arm.

'Let's try the ground floor first,' he said. 'Dining room, coffee shop, offices, whatever — '

She led the way to the door to the dining room, which was now barren of tables and chairs. They stopped at the entryway. 'What do you think — ?'

'Wait a minute,' Greg said. 'I hear voices.' He strode through the room, toward the swinging doors to the kitchen.

Tracy followed him. As soon as she entered, she felt her tension dissolve. Both Bill and Madeline were there, along with three young men, who were probably hotel employees. Madeline was picking up pots, pans and utensils from the floor, while the men struggled with the task of trying to raise a huge refrigerator that had toppled over. Greg went to join them, while Tracy hurried to Madeline's side. 'You're alive! I was so worried! I should have come over last night — '

Madeline forced a smile, but Tracy was appalled by her friend's looks. Her hair was a wild mess, and dirt streaked her face. The dress she wore was streaked with sand and dirt, so that its original color and pattern were almost totally obscured. Her hands and arms showed long scratches under their layer of grime.

'I didn't expect you to come,' Madeline said, the words coming out in almost breathless gasps. 'You have your own problems at the Breeze.'

'We're fine,' Tracy told her, stooping down and picking up spoons and ladles from the jumble of items on the floor. 'The tidal wave barely came up to our porch. But you . . . all those people in your lobby.'

'They're the last ones to check out. After the tidal wave last night, everyone who had been on the first floor and most of those on the second made a grand exodus. This is nothing by comparison.'

'No one was hurt?' Tracy asked.

'No,' Madeline said. 'Everyone was on the roof, and the third floor was spared; but it — ' She stopped, as if unable to describe the impact of the wave or the sensations that went through her when the wall of water slammed into them.

'The hotel — ' Tracy began.

'Still standing, as you see. The old girl did us proud. We haven't done a thorough investigation yet, but so far at least there doesn't seem to be any structural damage.'

By this time, the men had succeeded in righting the refrigerator. After instructing the others to check the enormous stoves and ovens, Bill joined. Tracy, who introduced Greg to Madeline. Bill looked as bedraggled as his fiancée, and his shirt was torn where he'd apparently caught it on something sharp.

'I know I shouldn't be here,' Tracy told Bill, 'but I had to see for myself if you and Madeline were all right. I was so worried — nobody's answering the phones.'

'We told the staff not to. There's no time. People are leaving in droves, checking out, trying to get refunds, trying to find other hotels, or flights back to the mainland. It's a zoo out there, I know, but we're doing the best we can.' He took a deep breath and went on. 'This is the most urgent. We have to make sure there are no gas leaks or water line breaks.'

'How long have you been here?' Tracy asked.

'Since we got everything back in order at the Ocean Breeze,' Bill answered.

'You mean since last night?' Greg's voice rose. 'No wonder you both look like death warmed over.'

Bill tried to smile, but his lips didn't move much, as if the effort was too much. 'Tell me about it,' he said.

'Look, you've got to get some rest. Let someone else do the dirty work.'

'I've got everyone slaving now. Someone has to — '

'Someone has to oversee it, I know,'

Tracy said. 'Let me do that, at least for awhile.'

Bill and Madeline both looked up at her in silence, and Greg added, 'I've been involved in hotel building and remodeling for years. Between us, we can hold down the fort for a few hours while you guys take a nap.'

'But we can't — ' Madeline started to say.

'You'll be able to think better once you're rested,' Tracy said. 'I know what needs to be done. Greg is on his way to Fiji, but I can handle things here for a few hours.'

'To hell with Fiji,' Greg said. 'You need all the hands you can get and mine are ready, willing and able.'

Bill shook his head. 'I don't know what to say.'

'Say you'll let us help.'

'Is there a bed still high and dry for you?' Tracy asked Madeline.

'Yes, on the third floor, I think.'

'I'll go back to the Breeze,' Bill said then. 'At least I'll be on the premises, even if I do fall asleep.'

'When your head hits the pillow, I have no doubt,' Greg told him.

Madeline arched her back, as if it ached from the constant stooping she'd been doing. 'I hope there's hot water. I need a shower before I climb into a bed.'

Ignoring the grime on Madeline's clothes, Tracy hugged her friend. 'Go along, now. We'll take care of things down here.'

Madeline and Bill pushed through the swinging doors and left the kitchen.

Tracy turned to Greg. 'Are you sure you want to do this? Catching a later flight is one thing, but this job may take all day.'

'Several days,' Greg corrected her, 'but I meant what I said. I don't have anything more useful to do. After all, that's what friends are for.'

'You met Bill only three days ago, and Madeline two minutes ago — '

'I make friends quickly, haven't you noticed?' He grinned at her, then turned serious. 'Let's get busy or the job will take more than just a few days.'

As Tracy headed for the lobby, her thoughts turned gloomy. Yes, they could clean up the sand and dirt in the hotel, but what about the ruined floors, and the possible wiring and plumbing problems? The tall, graceful palm trees and other plants, were undoubtedly in bad shape. And how about the swimming pool, the tennis courts? She hadn't been too sure Bill's inheritance would cover the improvements they wanted to make. Now, thanks to the tsunami, they were faced with a monumental restoration project. Almost as if it were her own problem, she again felt tears fill her eyes.

And then she remembered something. Insurance. Surely Madeline had some kind of insurance that would cover these expenses. With a lighter heart, she walked confidently back to the lobby to answer the constantly ringing telephones.

11

Greg threw his suitcase into the overhead bin and settled into his seat on the plane, heading for Fiji at last. He smiled to himself. He was two days late; that ought to upgrade the concept of Island Time. But of course, business-man that he was, he had telephoned that first day to change his appoint-ment.

Until now, the telephone call was the only time he'd thought about visiting the hotel on Fiji. The entire two days had been spent restoring the Island Sands to some sort of order. All through the first day, he and Tracy had worked together. She knew what needed to be done and delegated jobs to the hotel workers; he supervised the actual physical work and contributed his own manual labor. He'd found some heavy-duty overalls and put his good clothes in his car, then pitched in with all the energy he could summon. He'd thought he was in good shape — after all, he worked out at a gym three times a week — but nothing had prepared him for two days of clearing fallen trees, shoveling wet sand, lifting and moving heavy wooden or wrought iron furniture. Even after both Madeline and Bill returned to the Sands, Greg had stayed on, not willing to leave until order was restored.

Tracy, he knew, had done her share of heavy work that first day; but, on the second, when Bill and Madeline took over again, she had gone back to the Ocean Breeze to resume her duties as assistant manager. Many of the former guests of the Sands had checked into the Breeze after the tsunami, so that the hotel was fully occupied; she'd have plenty to do.

Tracy. The very thought of her made his pulse race. It wasn't just her blond hair, her creamy skin, the fabulous figure. Sure, he'd always been a sucker for a beautiful woman — what man wasn't? — but she exuded a particular warmth and charm. She was outgoing and friendly; and, even when she was giving orders, her manner was that of someone who respects others.

He leaned back against the headrest and closed his eyes, recalling images of Tracy on board the cruise ship when she tried to give him the lei. Then he thought of her in the hotel garden the next night and, finally, on the lanai after he'd pulled her from the grip of the tidal wave. He could almost feel her touch, the taste of her mouth. He'd get this mandatory trip out of the way and hurry back to her.

And then what? The voice inside reminded him that Tracy was not about to fall into his arms just because he wanted her. They had serious problems to overcome. First of all, in spite of the occasional lapse when she'd let him kiss her, she seemed to consider him an enemy simply because of the company he represented. What if Titan Industries decided to buy the Ocean Breeze? What if, just as she'd hinted, they decided to put in their own management team and fired her? She'd not only be out of a job, but would hate him for his part in it. He'd already hinted that he could steer Titan away from the Ocean Breeze — give it a negative report so they wouldn't be interested in buying it — but she wouldn't hear of it. She didn't want charity or lies, and he respected that. And liked her all the more because of it.

Even without that problem, she lived in Hawaii and he in California. She'd made it clear right from the start that she wasn't interested in a short-term relationship. Okay, so maybe he'd make it a long-term one; but not before they really knew each other. He wasn't about to make a second mistake like that. But how to get to know her better, when the business that was taking him to Fiji today would take him other places in the world all too soon?

To tell the truth, he wasn't all that

keen about working for Titan anymore. All the traveling was beginning to get him down. And Tracy hadn't needed to point out the ugliness of La Casa Grande in Mexico. He'd known it was a travesty from the moment he'd seen the architect's plans. But at the time, speaking his mind on such a matter hadn't been feasible; he'd needed the job. He'd been working for the Heritage Foundation before that. He liked the idea of saving historic buildings. However, since most of the organization's income came from grants and donations, the pay was abominably low, too low to suit his then wife. So Greg had signed on with Titan at a grand salary, and then she complained about the hours and the constant traveling. Just what did women want anyway?

But if he quit his job at Titan, then what? The type of work he did was specialized, not in great demand. Other companies who could use his services might be farther away or require even more traveling than he did now, not exactly conducive to getting to know Tracy better.

And then an idea struck. Why not help her look for work in California? She wanted to become a manager of a nice hotel. No sweat, he'd get her a job. He had contacts in the hotel business, several right in Los Angeles. Surely one of them wouldn't hesitate to hire such a charming, experienced young woman. She'd be grateful to him, and then —

Greg smiled more broadly, and his seatmate looked over at him, as if wondering what there was about the flight safety information on the video screen that made him so happy.

12

On Friday morning Tracy returned to the Island Sands, where she persuaded Madeline to take a break from her constant activity and have some breakfast.

'You have to keep up your strength,' she told her friend. 'You've been working like a slave for almost three days.'

Madeline brushed the hair out of her eyes. 'But there's still so much to be done.'

'Fifteen minutes won't make that much difference. But everything will go to pot if you faint from exhaustion and hunger.' She took Madeline's arm and led her gently toward the kitchen. 'Come on, let's have some coffee. I brought muffins.'

Madeline gave her a weak smile and followed; and, once in the kitchen, collapsed into a wooden chair at the table normally used by the cooks for their own meals. 'There's plenty of food here, you know. It was all carried up to the roof before the tsunami.'

'I know, but the bread and rolls are probably stale by now, and I doubt that you've ordered any fresh supplies.'

Madeline shrugged. 'That's true.'

'But at least the coffee urn is working,' Tracy said, pulling two mugs from an upper cabinet and pouring coffee for them both. She glanced briefly around the room — it was almost as sparkling as it had been before the tidal wave — then sat next to Madeline in one of the other wooden chairs.

'You've done a remarkable job already getting things in order,' Tracy said. 'I wouldn't have believed it when I saw the mess in here on Tuesday.'

'All the staff has been wonderful, and so was your friend Greg Thompson. His good ideas alone probably saved hours of work.'

'He's not my friend, remember?'

Tracy said. 'He's the man who's going to tell Titan Industries to buy the Ocean Breeze and force me out of a job.'

'You don't know that. Perhaps they won't buy it after all.' She took a bite of a banana muffin and chewed thoughtfully for a few moments. 'It's lucky I'm not trying to sell the Sands,' she added. 'I'd have a hard time persuading anyone it's a good investment right now.'

'But you and Bill were going to restore it anyway. Now you just have more of an incentive.'

'And more expenses than his inheritance can cover if it were four times as large.' Her lips began to tremble and she took a sip of coffee, as if to cover her distress.

Tracy reached across the table and squeezed Madeline's other hand. 'But you have insurance. Repairing damage like this is exactly what that flood insurance everyone had to buy is all about.'

'Assuming the insurance company follows through,' Madeline said.

Tracy felt her forehead pucker as she frowned. 'But surely they have to. Have you contacted them about it?'

'Of course. I called them the very first day.'

'And — ?' Tracy prompted.

Madeline's tone indicated her frustration. 'First it was impossible to get through on the telephone, then I was put on hold long enough to knit a sweater. They finally said someone would get back to me.' She paused to take a deep breath. 'That was the good news.'

'What do you mean?'

'The bad news is that they don't believe I'm insured. They can't find any record of me or the hotel.'

'But that's ridiculous,' Tracy protested. 'It's probably just a temporary computer glitch.' She had another thought. 'Don't you have a copy of the insurance papers?'

'I did once. Remember what my

office looked like on Tuesday? Every filing cabinet fell over, and every piece of paper in it was either turned into pulp or washed away when the tide retreated.'

Tracy tried to cheer her. 'It's not much consolation, but I suppose the insurance company has lots of claims to handle. Yours isn't the only one. It might take more time, but I'm sure that eventually it will all be cleared up. You'll have this old place restored to its former glory, and modernized besides.'

'Oh, Tracy, I hate to sound defeatist, but what do I do in the meantime? You were here right after this happened.' Madeline swept her arms around as if to encompass the entire hotel, not just the kitchen. 'You saw the people leaving. We not only have no income, but I had to return deposits.'

'You said the third floor was all right,' Tracy reminded her. 'Surely those people stayed.'

'Why should they? There was no service and everything was a total mess

— the swimming pool, the patios, everything on the first floor. I don't blame them, I wouldn't have stayed if I were in their shoes.'

'But now that you've cleaned it up so well and the — '

Madeline interrupted her. 'We've done a lot, but there's no way we can accept guests. And without guests we have no income. Did you notice the lobby floor? All the parquet is coming up, swollen from the water. Of course, parquet never should have been installed in the first place. Bill and I had planned to replace it with terrazzo.'

'A short delay,' Tracy said, trying to sound optimistic even though she knew the local workmen couldn't do a job like that very fast, even if they had no other work on the island, which they probably did, thanks to damage from the tidal wave.

'That's just the beginning,' Madeline was saying. 'The gardens will come back quickly, but several trees will have to be replaced and the pool may be damaged. In fact, the man is supposed to come out and check it this morning. And,' she added, angry now rather than weepy, 'all kinds of people are supposed to come and check the building for structural damage. We can't have guests in here if a wall or ceiling might collapse. Wiring may have to be replaced. And I have no income to pay anyone. We're already using Bill's extra money just to pay the staff.'

'But without guests, do you need the staff?'

'We've needed them for the clean-up, something the waiters never expected to have to do, I'm sure. But they've been wonderful about it,' she added. 'I'm going to hate to have to lay them off when we've done all we can do by ourselves.' She stopped and took a deep breath. 'I'm sorry, Tracy. I didn't mean to burden you with all my problems.'

'I just wish I could help.'

'You did more than enough that first day, and I'm encouraged just by the fact that you care. Maybe I'll lose the hotel, but I'll still have my health, and you for a friend. And Bill.'

Tracy mentally applauded Madeline's attitude, but her natural optimism wouldn't let her think that anything as serious as losing everything would actually happen. 'But you won't lose the hotel,' she said, her voice rising as if the volume would convince her friend. 'The insurance company will pay up. They have to. It will all work out, you'll see.'

Madeline finished her coffee, pushed the cup across the table and rose to her feet. 'I guess I don't really think I'll lose the hotel. But when I can't sleep at night, the thought crosses my mind.'

Tracy followed Madeline back toward the lobby. 'Besides Bill's inheritance, can't you get a bank loan while you're waiting for the insurance money?'

'I already have one of those, remember?'

'But once the hotel is remodeled, you'll be able to raise rates and keep it full besides. Surely the bank can see the potential for repaying the loans.'

'Who knows what bankers think? Naturally, I've been trying to reach them ever since this happened, but the right loan officer hasn't returned my calls. Meanwhile, Bill says we have to get estimates for everything that needs to be done, and until the experts get finished checking us out, we won't be able to do that.'

As they crossed the lobby, one of Tracy's sandals snagged on a piece of parquet that had popped up from the floor, and she started to fall. At once, Madeline reached out and caught her arm, steadying her. 'Do be careful,' she said. 'The floor is a hazard, which is another reason it's just as well we don't have any guests now. The last thing I need is for someone to fall down and sue me!'

A glance down at the uneven surface convinced Tracy that Madeline was right. She started for the entrance doors, placing her feet more carefully this time. 'I guess I'd better get back to my own job. But I wish there was something more I could do to help.'

'I'm afraid all we can do at the moment is wait.' Madeline gave a wry laugh. 'I've never been very good at that.' She paused, then added, 'Actually, there is something to do while we're waiting.'

Madeline's frown had turned into a smile, which, although Tracy thought it strange, she was glad to see.

'Bill and I are getting married,' Madeline said.

For a moment, the thought failed to register. When it did, Tracy threw her arms around her friend. 'Getting married? That's wonderful. When? Where? How?'

'One question at a time. We only decided late last night but it's going to be very simple, very cheap and very soon'

Tracy was thrilled. 'Can I help with that?'

'Of course. In fact, I want you to be my maid of honor. It's going to be the smallest wedding on record, so you and Bill's friend John are all the attendants we'll have. No bridesmaids, no grooms-men, just the four of us.'

'I know your mom and dad are gone, but don't you have brothers or sisters?'

'Two sisters. They're a lot older than I am. When Mom died, Dad decided to live his dream of owning a hotel in the tropics and brought me out here with him. I was seventeen.'

'But you've seen them since then?' Tracy asked.

'Of course. They both live in Virginia and have families, but they flew out here for a vacation once, and I went back there a few times.'

'They'll surely want to come out for your wedding.'

'I'll call and tell them, but I'm not optimistic they'll be able to make it. And I'm certainly not in a position to pay their way.'

'What about Bill's family?'

'Like you, he was an only child, but his parents retired here on the island a few years ago, so they'll come.'

'This is such good news,' Tracy said.

'I'm delighted you want me to stand up with you. When is the big day?'

'A week from tomorrow. We thought we'd do it in the wedding gazebo right here on the property.'

'Perfect. What shall I wear? What will you wear?'

'I'm going to go native, with a white muumuu, bare feet and flowers in my hair.'

Tracy laughed. 'I love it. I'll do the same, but not a white muumuu, of course.' She clutched Madeline's arm again. 'And what a super plan to have a wedding to occupy you while you're waiting for the renovation to get started.'

'I have to confess,' Madeline said, 'we had an ulterior motive for doing it now. The bank was never very happy about my taking over the hotel when my father died. They're a bunch of male chauvinist — well, you know what I mean. They didn't think a woman could run a business.'

'But you've done very well.'

'Yes, I've made the payments on time

every month, so they've had nothing to complain about. Until now.' She paused. 'But when Bill and I get married, he'll be joint owner and that may make them more reasonable about lending us enough money.'

'That sounds like a great idea.' Tracy paused and grinned. 'Good thing you and Bill just happen to love each other.'

'Ah, love,' Madeline said. 'Without Bill's love, I don't think I could have gotten through this catastrophe at all. Together, I feel as if we'll make it.'

'Oh, you will,' Tracy said, 'you will. With flying colors!'

After a last hug, she left the building and walked quickly up the road toward the Ocean Breeze. Thoughts of the coming wedding swirled through her head and she remembered Madeline's words about loving Bill. Suddenly she felt a stab of envy. For the moment at least she still had her job, but it would be nice to be like Madeline and Bill. To love someone with all her heart and soul — and have him love her back.

13

The wedding gazebo at the Island Sands stood atop a small hill behind a rock-lined waterfall just beyond the broad patio at the beach side of the hotel. Screened by fan-shaped palms, hibiscus and bird of paradise plants, only the white latticed roof was visible from the garden paths, giving the entire scene a sense of privacy.

Tracy had joined Madeline, Bill and the minister on the small round platform the night before, while rehearsing for the wedding. At first, Bill had questioned the need for a rehearsal; but his parents insisted they have one and, since they were paying all the wedding expenses, he decided to go along with their request.

'Since we're doing this on the cheap,' Bill had said, 'I guess I can let them help.'

Now, Saturday afternoon, Tracy joined Madeline in one of the third floor rooms of the hotel. Madeline had already donned her wedding gown, a long, full-skirted white muumuu of softest cotton with lace inserts at the square neckline, elbow-length sleeves and a bottom ruffle. Flat white slippers covered her feet.

Tracy pulled off the dress she'd worn on her trip from the Ocean Breeze, and donned a silk slip before putting on a long sleeveless dress of sheer voile. The fabric, printed in muted shades of pinks, purples and blues, looked as if someone had painted flowers on it and then left it out in the rain so the water could blend and soften the colors.

'Oh, you look so lovely,' Madeline said.

'Me? You're the lovely one, a truly beautiful bride. And your dark hair is such a wonderful contrast to your dress.' She paused and looked around the room. 'Where are the flowers?'

'In that box.' Madeline pointed to a

long florist's box resting on one of the two double beds in the room.

Tracy lifted the lid and brought out a delicate circlet of white orchids and ginger blossoms, and at once a delicious perfume filled the air. She placed it on her friend's hair and forehead, Hawaiian style. 'Perfect.' Then she put on her own circlet of pale orchids and plumeria.

Next, she retrieved the maile — an open lei of green vines intertwined with tiny, velvety pikake blossoms — and draped it over Madeline's shoulders, where it fell almost to her knees on either side.

Madeline fingered the petals. 'Did you know that the figurative meaning of 'lei' is 'beloved'? I read it in a Hawaiian dictionary once. It said, 'a beloved child was carried on the shoulders, with its legs draped down on both sides, like the open lei.''

'What a lovely thought,' Tracy said.

Tracy returned to the florist's box and pulled out a small bouquet of white orchids for Madeline to carry, and one of pink carnations for herself. 'I think we're ready,' she said.

'Oh, is it time?' Madeline stepped over to the full-length mirror on the back of the bathroom door and took a last look at herself. 'I can't believe this is really happening. I feel as if that's some other woman staring back at me.'

Tracy laughed and hugged Madeline briefly, careful not to crush their flowers, and then opened the door to the hall.

They swept down its length to the grand staircase, whose worn carpeting had been covered with a new white runner, and descended to the first floor. Careful to step only where parquet had been removed, temporarily replaced by carpet, they crossed the lobby and went out the open patio doors. Friends and hotel employees lined the path to the gazebo, and four young men, wearing brightly-printed short-sleeved shirts, played Hawaiian music on guitars and ukuleles.

When they reached the steps leading to the ceremony platform, Bill, grinning from ear to ear, stepped forward and took Madeline's arm. He wore a white shirt that showed off his deep tan, black pants, red satin cummerbund and a maile of vines across his shoulders. Tracy stepped in front of them, next to John Nakamoto, Bill's best man, and together, they led the way up the stairs.

On the wedding platform, Tracy and John walked toward the minister, then stepped to opposite sides to let the bride and groom stand in front. The music stopped and the minister began. 'We are gathered together — '

The beauty of the moment almost brought tears to Tracy's eyes, but then her thoughts flew to Greg. Where was he? On one of his many telephone calls to her during the past week — during which she had told him about Madeline and Bill's decision to be married right away — he had assured her he would return to Honolulu in time for the wedding, but she'd heard nothing from him since Wednesday night. Had his business kept him away? Had he changed his mind?

Forced to keep her eyes forward, she wasn't able to scan the guests and she was pretty sure he hadn't been anywhere on the path leading to the gazebo. Because of his height, he would likely have stood out from most of the others. Tracy made a conscious effort not to frown. This was Madeline and Bill's big moment, and she was happy for them. She wouldn't let her disappointment over Greg's apparent absence overshadow that.

And why was she feeling upset anyway? She certainly didn't wish she and Greg were the happy couple listening to marriage vows. How many times had she told herself that they could never be more than friends? Still, when he had phoned, usually late at night when she was already in her room getting ready for bed, they had talked for a long time: she telling him of the progress cleaning up the Sands, he telling her amusing stories about his visits to other hotels and resorts. He described the people he met sometimes in not-so-flattering terms, and made every incident seem amusing, if not exciting. He not only cheered her up, but also made her feel as if they had known each other for years instead of only days.

Almost before she knew it the brief ceremony was over. Bill and Madeline kissed, then turned and descended the steps of the gazebo. As she followed, Tracy's gaze darted about. She hoped to see Greg among the guests, but it wasn't until she spotted someone with a video recorder obscuring most of his face, that she realized he was there and taping the event.

As if he understood she had recognized him, he put up one hand in a salute, and then hurried to keep ahead of the bride and groom. They were heading for the beach, running and laughing, while the guests ran alongside, throwing flower petals in their path.

When they reached the sand, Madeline and Bill both slipped out of their shoes and began to run up the beach. Greg followed them, filming as he went. Soon several people were pulling off their shoes and running across the sand, women holding up their dresses as they dashed in and out of the gentle waves of the blue Pacific.

Tracy stepped out of her own shoes and did the same, her hands grasping her skirt to keep it dry. The musicians had followed too, now playing a lively tune, and soon everyone was dancing in the sand, laughing and singing. This time tears ran down Tracy's cheeks, tears of happiness for her two friends at this perfect moment.

* * *

Darkness found everyone still sitting on woven mats on both sides of a long table in the grassy garden courtyard. Covered with ti leaves and palm fronds, it held a fabulous assortment of island food for the wedding luau. Someone had dug a pit and roasted a pig in it earlier that day and now what was left of the main course sat in the center of the table, an apple still in its mouth. They had also devoured most of the lomi lomi salmon, rice, vegetables and fruit, and now a large coconut cake was cut and served. Tracy accepted a small piece, although she felt quite stuffed already.

'It's wedding cake,' Greg told her, handing her a clean fork. 'You have to have some.' He had long since shed both his shoes and jacket, removed his tie, opened his top shirt buttons and rolled up his sleeves, as had all the other men in the party who weren't wearing Hawaiian shirts. Still, he looked handsome and as well-groomed as ever. Tracy decided that he'd probably look elegant in anything he wore, even a bathrobe and slippers.

She took the plate from him and sampled the cake. It was tender, sweet and delicious. Greg tasted his and then picked up his camera again and filmed Madeline and Bill feeding pieces of cake to each other.

'I hope they don't smear their faces with it,' Greg said. 'I hate that.'

'Me, too. I don't know how that custom began but I think it's crude and disrespectful.'

Faces clean, except for bits of icing at the corners of their mouths, Madeline and Bill picked up their glasses of wine and, arms entwined, drank from the other's glass. John Nakamoto stood up, raising his glass of wine and proposed a toast to the bride and groom. Then Tracy did the same, citing her admiration and love for both Madeline and Bill. That was followed by a toast from Bill's father and several other people who had special ties to the couple. Finally, Madeline and Bill stood up and thanked everyone. Then, as if on cue, a small group of musicians and dancers appeared on the patio behind them and filled the air with the sound of drums and the rattle of gourds, as they performed the Hawaiian hula and Tahitian dances.

Greg, who had continued to film during the toasts, added only a few minutes of the entertainment to the taping, and then put down the camera once more.

'I think it's wonderful that you brought a video camera. The tape will be a great gift for Madeline and Bill.'

'I only thought of it at the last minute,' he said, 'as I was getting off the plane. I had to fill out seventy-five forms and swear to give them my firstborn son in order to rent the thing and it made me too late to change clothes.'

Tracy grinned. 'What? You didn't dress up especially for the occasion?'

Greg spoke in a Western drawl. 'These are my workin' duds, ma'am. I'da changed before gettin' on the plane, but didn't have no time no-how.'

Tracy laughed, then glanced away just in time to see Bill help Madeline to her feet. The couple began to walk hand in hand back toward the hotel.

Greg apparently noticed their departure as well. 'Are they staying here tonight?' he asked Tracy.

'No, they're in the bridal suite at the Ocean Breeze. But that's a secret,' she added. 'Promise you won't tell.'

He raised one hand as if in a Boy Scout oath. 'I promise.' He lowered his hand and caught one of Tracy's in it. 'Can we take a walk on the beach? I've eaten far too much myself and need to get a little exercise.'

Tracy looked around. 'I guess so. I don't think I'm needed anymore. Bill's parents insisted on hiring a caterer to prepare the food and clean up afterward.'

'If they hadn't, would you be doing K.P.?'

'Definitely.' She laughed. 'I'd probably have helped dig the pit, cook the rice, cut up mountains of fruit and even baked the cake!'

Greg helped her to her feet, and led her toward the path to the beach. 'I'm impressed that you know how to do all that. Can you make poi, too?'

'I didn't say I could really do it,' she said. 'And I don't even eat poi.'

'I tried some,' Greg said. 'It tastes suspiciously like library paste.'

Tracy laughed again. 'I tried it when I first arrived here myself, and I find it more like gooey mashed potatoes without any salt or other seasoning. Too bland.'

'So you like spicy food?'

'No, not really. But, in my opinion, a little salt makes a lot of things palatable.'

Tracy's shoes were still lying somewhere in the garden, and she stepped out on the sand barefoot. Greg had also left his shoes and socks elsewhere and now he rolled up his pants legs to his knees. He lifted his head and sniffed the sea air coming to them on a gentle breeze. 'Ah, that feels good.'

The breeze swirled Tracy's skirt around her legs and lifted her hair slightly above her neck. 'A perfect end to a perfect day,' she said. 'No wonder they call this place Paradise.'

Greg stopped walking and turned to her. 'And do you never want to leave?'

'Who would?'

'Well, most people in the world actually live somewhere else, you know. Places like, oh, say, Los Angeles.'

'Los Angeles? With its smog and traffic and crime?' She kept walking up the beach and Greg matched his stride to hers.

'Don't believe everything you hear,' he said. 'Yes, there's a lot of traffic, but smog is way down from what it used to be, and so is crime.' He paused. 'And don't tell me there's no crime in Hawaii; I read the papers and watch the evening news, you know.'

'Okay, so we have our share, but think of the weather. Sunshine every day, temperatures in the seventies or eighties, not nineties or hundreds, no horrible humidity.'

'But Southern California is a lot like that. You mustn't compare it to Chicago summers.'

Tracy shrugged. 'Okay, I suppose you're right. Since I haven't lived anywhere but Chicago and here, I guess I shouldn't judge.'

'There are places with beautiful weather all over the globe. Australia has them, and Japan, France, Italy, Greece — '

'All right, already, you've convinced me. But I'm living here now and I love it, so I don't care about those other places.'

They walked in silence for a while, the only sound being the clack-clack of palm fronds stirred by the breeze, and Tracy wondered why Greg seemed preoccupied.

Finally he said, 'What will you do if my company does decide to buy the Ocean Breeze and you lose your job? Try to find another in Hawaii? Go back to Chicago?'

'I'd never go back to Chicago,' she said vehemently. 'Yes, I'd try to find another here. It might mean working my way up the ladder again, but it would be worth it, I think.'

'Suppose I were to suggest coming to Los Angeles? I know lots of hotel owners and managers. I think I could find a place for you.'

Tracy stopped walking and turned to him. 'It's settled then, isn't it? I suppose this is your way of breaking it to me gently. Titan's going to buy the hotel and toss me out, so you're dangling another job in front of my eyes to soften the blow.'

'No, that's not it at all,' he said. 'I haven't heard a word from them about their plans. Actually, I'm still submitting information about some of the other hotels I've visited. I checked out several on both Maui and Kauai that might do very well. Besides, they're only interested in acquiring one hotel at this time.'

Tracy moved slowly toward the water's edge, letting the cool waves lap at her toes, feeling the sand sink under her feet. The ocean was silver over black, the sky dark blue with a sliver of a crescent moon. 'When will you be finished? When can I expect the axe to fall?'

'*If* it falls,' Greg said. 'And it may not. I only made the offer of a position in L.A. because I hate the idea of leaving here myself.'

Tracy felt her heartbeat accelerate. Did he mean leaving *her*? Had the chemistry they felt between them grown into something more for him, as it had for her?

He answered her unspoken question by coming close, putting his arms around her and looking deeply into her eyes. 'Tracy, I can't bear the thought of never seeing you again. I know you need time to get over that guy in Chicago; but if you came to L.A. we could see each other often. We'd find out if this is the real thing.'

'And if it's not, then I'd have to leave L.A., just as I left Chicago.' She thought of telling him that she'd been terribly hurt and was only just beginning to trust again; that he, Gregory

Thompson, apparently had the power to break through the barrier she'd put up around herself. Part of her wanted him to tear down her defenses, but the other part knew how foolish that would be.

A wave splashed over her ankles and Tracy pulled back from the water. 'What if you discover I'm not the person you think I am?'

'So I'd have made another mistake. I told you I'm divorced. I was thirty and my company preferred its employees to get married and have families. I met someone I thought would be compatible and persuaded myself that I could love her. I was wrong.'

He reached for Tracy again. 'But I didn't leave anyone with a broken heart. I would have stuck with the marriage, even without the love I knew I was missing; but she wasn't fooled. She said my long working hours and constant traveling told her plainly that I didn't need her in my life. She found someone else in record time and we divorced with mutual feelings of relief.'

'I'm happy for you that it worked out so harmoniously, but that doesn't mean — '

He interrupted her with a kiss. His lips were smooth and firm, and then, after a moment, she put her arms around him and felt the same comfort and warmth that she had when he'd saved her from the tidal wave.

When they pulled apart, he said, 'Tracy, I have a very strong feeling that this time I'm not making a mistake.'

She stepped out of his arms. 'I think you're letting the magic of Hawaii influence you. The sun, the flowers, the romance of the islands have made fools of people before. No one is immune. Not even you.' She turned and walked briskly back in the direction of the hotel.

'You're wrong,' he said, following her. 'I'll prove it to you. Somehow.'

She didn't look back. She wanted to believe him, but too many obstacles stood in their path, not the least of them being that she refused to let herself be hurt again. She would be very sure next time before she allowed herself to love someone.

Yet, she found her eyes misting and her throat tightening. If Greg *was* the right man for her, why did he have to live so far away? Why did they have so little time to get to know each other?

14

Tracy was dragged from sleep the next morning by the ringing of her telephone. Still groggy, she reached out for the instrument and pulled it into the bed with her, cradling it between her head and the pillow. 'Hello?'

'Sorry to wake you.' The voice on the other end was male and familiar: her father. She opened her eyes. The room was still dark, the digital clock on the nightstand read four-fifteen.

'Dad! Have you forgotten about the time difference?' In spite of the hour, she managed to put a chuckle into her voice.

'Oh — Well, yes, I guess I have.'

The long silence on her father's part set Tracy's thoughts racing. He knew there was a four-hour time difference between Chicago and Hawaii in the winter and five in the summer, when most of the mainland went on daylight savings time; he wouldn't have forgotten that. Something was wrong.

She pulled herself up to her elbows, brushing the hair from her forehead with one hand. 'What is it, Dad? What's happened?' Her heart had begun to pound and she felt too hot under the sheet and single thermal blanket on the bed.

'It's your mom. She's had an accident.'

Tracy instantly pictured a car crash: crumpled vehicles on the side of the road, red police car lights swirling, the 'jaws of life' desperately trying to free a body from the wreckage. Her throat tightened and she could hardly speak. 'Is she — ?'

'I didn't mean to upset you. I should have waited to call. But this happened last night and — '

'Dad,' Tracy almost screamed into the telephone, 'tell me what happened. Is she all right?'

'Of course she is. She just slipped on

some ice and broke her leg.'

Tracy felt her breath return. 'Oh, Dad, you shouldn't scare me like that.' She paused. 'Not that this isn't bad enough. Is she in the hospital?'

'No, she's at home now. But she's sort of helpless, both her right arm and her right leg are in casts.'

'Her arm *and* her leg? I thought you said she just broke her leg?'

'Well, at first that's all we thought was wrong; but when we got to the hospital, they took a lot of X-rays and found she'd broken her arm, too.'

'Oh, Dad, that *is* a problem. She's right-handed.' Then Tracy remembered something else. Her mom and dad had a small business they ran by themselves, a stationery store. Her mother worked in it almost as many hours as her dad. 'What about the store?' she asked.

'Well, now, that is a problem. I'm not sure what we'll do.'

'*I* know what you'll do,' Tracy said. She flung the covers off and swung her legs over the side of the bed. 'You'll get my old bedroom ready and meet me at the airport when I fly in.'

'But you can't just — '

'Of course I can, Dad. You need me and I'll take some vacation time or just a leave of absence, it doesn't matter. But I'm coming, so don't argue.'

As she listened to her father express his gratitude for her decision, she cradled the phone between her neck and head and began to wriggle out of her nightgown. 'I'll call you as soon as I have some flight information,' she told him. 'Stay near the phone for the next hour or so.'

'I will. Thanks, honey. I love you.'

'I love you, too, Dad.'

Suddenly the joy she felt at the opportunity to see her parents again began to shrivel. They weren't the only people who lived in Chicago. Paul lived there, too. What if she ran into him again?

★ ★ ★

It was dark when Tracy stepped out of the terminal at O'Hare that evening. And cold. She pulled the heavy navy-blue jacket — the same one she'd worn the day she left Chicago three months before — more tightly around her body and tried to scrunch her neck into its collar. Fortunately, she didn't have to wait long. She saw her father's white Oldsmobile moving slowly along the curb. When he saw her he stopped the car, popped open the trunk and got out.

'Where's your luggage?' he asked, hugging her at the same time.

'I only brought this tote bag,' Tracy said, lifting it up. 'I hope Mom didn't throw away that box of winter clothes I gave her when I moved.'

'You know your mom,' he said. 'When did she ever throw away anything?'

They laughed and got into the car, and as they drove toward Evanston, Tracy asked for details about the accident. Her father explained how her

185

mother had slipped and fallen on a patch of icy sidewalk as they'd left a movie theater.

When they arrived at the Colonial style two-story house, Tracy hurried to the master bedroom, where her mother was propped up in bed, wearing a pink ruffled bed jacket and a pink bow in her blond hair.

'Oh, Mom,' Tracy said, leaning over and kissing her on both cheeks. 'You look — darling.'

Karen Barnes laughed. 'Oh, you mean the ribbon. Rebecca Robinson from next door — you remember her — came over today and fixed my hair. I haven't quite mastered doing it with my left hand yet.'

Tracy examined the cast on her mother's arm and pulled down the sheet and blanket to see the one on her leg. 'You really did it, didn't you? You took a trip that cost you an arm and a leg!'

They both laughed at that, and then her mother said, 'I never fall on the ice,

I'm so used to it. I can't imagine how it happened this time.' She paused. 'I'm so glad you've come. You really shouldn't have, you know. I'm taking you away from your job. They won't fire you, will they?'

'Not over this.' Tracy sat on the edge of the bed and told her mother about Greg Thompson's company possibly buying the Ocean Breeze hotel and putting someone else in her place. She didn't mention that she and Greg were tremendously attracted to each other; but something in her voice must have alerted her mother to the possibility of romance, because she brought up the subject of Madeline and Bill.

'The last time you called, you mentioned your friends were going to get married. When's the wedding?' her mother asked.

'It was yesterday, as a matter of fact.'

'Tell me about it.'

'Mom, it's very late and I'm sure you need some rest. Let's save that for tomorrow.'

'Did it give you any ideas about a wedding of your own someday?'

Tracy chuckled. 'You're just like mothers everywhere, wanting to see your daughter get married. And here I thought you were different. Next thing I know you'll be saying you want me to give you some grandchildren.'

'I'm just being normal.'

'Well, you have to give me some time. I've only been in Hawaii three months, hardly enough time to meet anyone, much less think about marriage.' Her conscience pricked. She was talking as if she wanted a man in her life, but she couldn't tell her mother the truth — that her experience with Paul had soured her on the whole idea.

Fortunately, her mother changed the subject. 'You really like living in Hawaii, don't you?'

'Even more than I thought I would. You and Dad ought to retire and move out there, too. Bill's folks live there, and they love it.'

'Well, perhaps, someday,' her mother

said. 'But we're not ready to retire. Your Dad's only fifty-two and I'm still in my forties, at least for another year. And right now we still have the store to run. Since I'm totally out of commission, you'll have your hands full.'

'I don't mind.' Tracy got up and kissed her mother again. 'It's late and you need your rest. See you in the morning.'

★   ★   ★

Tracy had asked for a month's leave, which meant that Bill, although officially resigned from his position at the Ocean Breeze, had resumed his position as manager while they waited to learn Titan Industries' decision about buying the hotel.

Greg had insisted on taking Tracy to the airport, telling her he had to go there anyway to fly to Los Angeles that day; and he had kissed her soundly at the boarding gate. 'I'll miss you terribly,' he'd said. 'Absence makes the heart grow fonder, you know.'

'But,' she chided him, 'isn't there another proverb that says, out of sight, out of mind?'

'They're not necessarily contradictory. Think of time as a wind, and love as a flame. The wind will put out a small flame, but make a big one grow brighter.' He grinned. 'I expect the wind of this absence to fan mine into a raging forest fire.'

She thought of his words often during the next few days. In fact, he hardly let her forget them, since he called her from Los Angeles almost every night at ten o'clock, just as he had when she was still in Honolulu and he was on other islands. She began to anticipate his calls and retired to her room by that time so she could lie across her bed and talk to him. He told her about what he was doing now that he was back in his office, the people he worked with — always making them sound interesting — and he turned every incident into something amusing.

They talked about movies or current television shows. And they both loved to read so they discussed the books they'd bought and complained about not having enough time to read them.

He talked more about his travels as a youth, and she found herself telling him things about her own childhood that she hadn't discussed with anyone before. 'My father didn't move around like yours did,' she told him, 'so the most exciting thing I ever did was go to a cottage on a lake in Indiana every summer. I learned to swim, dive and water ski, but that's all.'

'By yourself? You said you were an only child.'

'Yes, but my father and my uncle bought the summer cottage together, so I had cousins to play with when we were there.'

'And in the winters?' Greg prompted.

'I went ice skating a few times but didn't like it. It was too cold. My fingers and toes got frostbitten. I guess

191

I've always known I belong in a warm climate.'

'So how is the weather there now?'

'Cold.' She laughed. 'I don't go out any more than I have to, just back and forth between here and the store.'

'Have your parents always owned the stationery store?'

'No, my dad was an accountant for a big Chicago company. But when they merged with another firm, he was offered an early-retirement package. He was too young to do nothing, so he bought the store and he and Mom have been running it ever since. It's perfect for them, because they both love dealing with people.'

'Just like their daughter,' Greg said.

Tracy grinned. 'Yes, I do like working with people. And the hotel business is even better than owning a store, because there's always someone new to meet.' She paused. 'I've met so many lovely people, and they often tell me to be sure to look them up if ever I'm in New Jersey or Idaho, or wherever.'

'I'll bet you could stay in a different town every night for a year, just visiting people you've met. I'll bet you keep in touch with them, too.'

'Well,' Tracy admitted, 'I do send a few Christmas cards. And now that I'm in Hawaii, I'm thinking of telling them to be sure to visit me at the Ocean Breeze.'

'Drumming up business? They'll have to pay you extra for that.'

'Speaking of the Ocean Breeze,' Tracy said, 'has Titan Industries decided about buying the hotel?'

'No word yet,' he told her. 'Believe me, I'll call you as soon as I know. By the way, what about the Island Sands? Did they get that insurance mess straightened out?'

'I haven't talked to Madeline much since I've been here. The time difference throws us off, and the last two times I tried, Madeline and Bill were out. She doesn't return my calls, even when I tell her to call collect.'

'If they're too busy to call you, that

must mean things are moving along with their renovation. With everything they have to do, they could be putting in twenty-hour days. I've done that myself — once or twice.'

'I suppose you're right.'

'I'd go over and check it out for you,' Greg said, 'but I want to postpone an unauthorized trip until you're there. You have to be sure to let me know when you plan to fly back so I can meet you at the airport.'

'Greg, you don't have to do that.'

'I'd come to Chicago to see you,' he added, 'but I can't justify a business trip in that direction, and I'm saving my vacation for when you and I can spend a lot of time together.'

'Even when I'm back, I won't have free time. I'm spending *my* vacation time right now, you know.'

'We'll work something out,' he said. 'Love will find a way.'

There was that 'love' word again. Tracy felt her face grow warm and didn't answer. She wouldn't let herself think of that now. All she wanted to do was get back to her job. She knew for sure that she loved the hotel business; but, as for Greg, maybe he was right for her and maybe he wasn't.

15

Because Greg phoned her every night, Tracy began to feel as though she were spending her evenings with him. For hours afterward, she thought about him, wondered what their future held. It had been different with Paul. They had met, dated, seemed to have a lot in common. One thing just sort of led to another and she'd begun to think of marriage. But he hadn't wanted what she did. Then Greg came along, bringing her doubt and confusion about what direction her life should take.

During the day, she managed to push him out of her mind. She and her father took turns at the store and at home. Her life took on a routine of selling merchandise, handling the bookkeeping, and helping her mother. Tracy, of course, also ended up doing most of the

cooking. Although she'd never considered herself good at it, she found the
box of three-by-five cards that contained her mother's favorite recipes and
managed to follow directions to everyone's satisfaction.

It was on a Saturday morning, after
she'd been home three weeks, that she
answered the front doorbell and found
Paul McCandless standing in front of
her.

'Paul.' She said his name and then
nothing. She stood motionless, wishing
she had somehow anticipated this moment
and rehearsed what she'd say to him.

'Hi.' He, too, seemed at a loss for
words. Finally, he loosened the knitted
wool scarf from around his neck and
cleared his throat. 'I heard you were
back in town.'

'Oh?' She wondered how he'd heard,
then remembered that sometimes people
from her former office came into the
stationery store. One of them must have
seen her working there and passed on
the news.

'It's only temporary,' she told him. 'My mom had an accident and I'm just filling in for a while.'

'How long do you think you'll be here?'

'A few more weeks.'

'You're not back for good?' After saying it, he looked down at his shoes, as if not really wanting to see her reaction to his question.

She didn't answer, suddenly conscious that she was making him stand on the front porch in the cold March wind. 'I'm sorry, I'm being rude. Come in. Would you like a cup of coffee?'

He entered and closed the door behind him. 'That would be nice. Thanks.'

She preceded him into the living room, then excused herself to go to the kitchen. Her thoughts swirled in confusion: Why had he come to see her? How should she react? She'd already invited him in and their conversation so far was that of polite strangers, not the romantic couple they'd once been. She decided to keep it on that level. She poured coffee into two of her mother's whimsical mugs, placed them on a tray and carried them into the living room.

Paul stood up briefly as she came in. He'd taken off his overcoat and was wearing a thick, dark green sweater over a flannel shirt and corduroy trousers. Never very heavy, he now seemed thinner than ever. His winter-pale face, also thin, made his nose seem prominent, his eyes large and round.

Tracy set the tray down on the coffee table and sat on the end of the sofa in front of it. After a moment's hesitation, Paul sat down on the other end.

'I believe you like it black,' Tracy said.

'You remembered?'

She felt some annoyance at his question. 'It hasn't been that long. Of course I remember.'

'It seems like forever to me.'

Uh-oh. What was that supposed to mean? Tracy felt her cheeks get warm and took a sip of coffee to cover her confusion.

Paul shifted his body until he was almost facing her. 'I suppose this isn't the right time or place, but I couldn't wait. The minute I heard you were here, I decided to come.' He paused, then his words rushed out as if he had a deadline to keep. 'I know that I made a terrible mistake by letting you go. I realize now that I love you and want to m —'

Tracy interrupted him, not wanting to hear the rest of his sentence. 'It's been almost four months. You didn't call or write. I'm sure you could have found out how to reach me if you really wanted to.'

He leaned forward, his hand on the sofa cushion between them. 'You can't imagine how many times I fantasized about calling you. But I wasn't sure what to say or how to say it. I'm not good at that. I even tried writing my thoughts but I always tore up the letters. They sounded too juvenile, too desperate. When I heard you were back, I felt as if my prayers had been answered.'

The sincerity in his voice touched Tracy's heart. Memories of being with him rushed back and made her hands tremble.

After a long silence, Paul spoke again. 'You aren't saying anything. Am I making a fool of myself?'

'I don't know what to say,' she told him. 'I've been leading a different life in Hawaii. Oh, the job is similar, but the surroundings, the weather, the people — ' A vision of Greg flashed before her eyes.

'You've forgotten me already, then.'

'No, not forgotten.' She searched for a word for how she felt, how the memories he'd evoked were pleasant but no longer compelling. 'Healed.'

'Healed?' His voice took on a stronger, injured tone. 'You make it sound as if I were a disease.'

'Falling in love with someone can be like that. It consumes us. It takes over all our thoughts, makes us do crazy things.'

'We never did anything crazy.'

'No.' She drank the rest of her coffee, then set the cup back on the coffee table. 'As I recall that was pretty much the point of our breaking up.'

'I wanted us to live together,' Paul said. 'You wanted to get married.'

She didn't look at him. 'It seemed like a good idea at the time.'

'And now?'

She turned to him. 'Are you asking me to marry you now? Is that what you started to say before?'

Paul put his cup down, cleared his throat, and then looked intently into her face. 'Yes. If that's the only way I can have what we had before, then yes.'

'What did we have before?'

'We did things together. We had fun, we were compatible.'

'We went to plays and films, the opera, the ballet. You were good company.' So what was different about her relationship with Greg? 'But I know

now,' she told Paul, 'that we were only friends.'

'We were more than that.'

'I used to think so, but I don't anymore. We never did anything crazy because we were never really in love.' Tracy remembered something Greg had said to her. 'I wanted to be married, and I persuaded myself that I loved you. I was wrong.'

'No, you were right. You did love me. We loved each other.' He grabbed her hands and tried to pull her to him.

She resisted the move, freed her hands and stood up. 'I've had time to think about this, too. The pain I felt then didn't last as long as I thought it would.' The thought of Greg intruded again, but she forced it away. She knew she wasn't in the process of switching her affections from one man to another. 'I have a career that means a lot to me. I love what I'm doing now, and I love where I'm doing it. I don't need a man to make my life complete.'

Paul had risen when she did, and

now he moved around the coffee table to the chair on which he'd placed his coat and scarf. After putting them on, he turned to her. 'I'm sorry. I guess I did make a fool of myself after all.'

'No, Paul. It's never foolish to dream of loving someone. I'm just not the right person for you. We should be grateful we found out before we made each other miserable.'

He put his hand out, as if to shake hers, then seemed to think better of it and withdrew it. He turned and went out of the room. She followed him through the hall and said good-bye as he opened the front door. Paul turned his head briefly, said, 'Goodbye' so softly she almost didn't hear it, and left.

Tracy stood in the hallway for a few moments, rehearsing what they'd said, especially her own words. She knew she'd done the right thing. The doubts she'd had when she first moved to Hawaii had dissolved at last.

16

Tracy felt a slight bump as the plane touched down at Honolulu airport and then, after they'd taxied to the terminal and the Fasten Seat Belt sign went off, she pulled out her tote bag and headed for the exit. She felt as if she'd been gone longer than thirty-seven days. But the trip had been necessary, and now her mother was back working in the stationery store and getting around quite well at home.

Tracy wished she could say the same for Madeline. The last she'd heard, the insurance matter still wasn't completely settled, and the knowledge disturbed her. She wished there was something she could do to help, but couldn't think of a thing besides offer moral support. Deep down, she couldn't imagine that this state of affairs could continue much longer.

And, although Madeline hadn't come right out and said so, Tracy assumed that they'd gone forward with the most pressing of the renovation projects at the Island Sands.

When she stepped out of the terminal, she looked around only briefly before Greg ran toward her.

'Tracy, am I glad to see you!'

He'd been right; this absence *had* made her heart grow fonder. The very sight of him made it beat wildly. His thick dark hair that she always wanted to touch, his strong chin, his lips, everything about him made her head reel.

He threw his arms around her and kissed her. Then, after she dropped her tote bag on the sidewalk so she could slip out of her heavy jacket, he swept her into his arms and kissed her again. Her thoughts swirled around in her head; she didn't want to let him see how much she cared, but at the same time she longed to melt against him and never let him go. Was this love?

Now that she knew for certain that Paul had no place in her life, had she fallen in love with Greg?

She thought her sudden new feelings must show in her face, and she felt it grow warmer. Flustered, she managed at least to smile at him. 'Thanks for picking me up.'

He propelled her to the curb, where a red Miata convertible waited, and helped her inside. 'Wild horses couldn't have kept me away.' He closed the car door, went around to the other side and got in. 'I've got two days to be with you and I plan never to let you out of my sight.'

His words made her tingle again, but she forced herself to be realistic. 'But that isn't possible. After the lengthy leave of absence I've just had, I need to put in lots of time at the hotel.'

'Bill isn't a slave driver. He'll let you have some time off to be with me.' He turned and grinned at her. 'I've already asked him.'

'You and Bill have become very

chummy, haven't you? When did this happen?'

'I guess while we were working together after the tsunami.'

'I'm glad you two hit it off. He's a wonderful guy and he's been a kind and generous boss to me; but I don't want to take advantage of his good nature by leaving him in the lurch again.'

'Not to worry. When I arrived from L.A. last night, I told him my plans and he said there'd be no problem.'

'And just what are these plans of yours?'

'To take you to Kauai to see Waimea Canyon and the Fern Grotto.'

He wanted to take her to Kauai? For how long? He'd indicated he had two days to spend with her. If that meant spending the night together on the other island, she'd — She didn't let herself think of it. She had to head him off, at least until she knew where their relationship was going. What if he didn't love her? Men often *acted* as if they were in love when it was only lust.

'Greg, I can't. Don't you understand?'

'Just one day,' he said, interrupting her. 'We fly out in the morning and back in time for dinner.'

'Even so — '

'No more arguments, it's all settled.'

Tracy looked straight out the windshield. 'We'll see about that. I'm going to ask Bill myself.'

'No problem. I told him we'd all have dinner together tonight.' He glanced over at her. 'That is, unless you had dinner on the plane.'

Tracy relaxed a little. 'They served something, but it was a long flight and I'm famished.'

They talked about the rest of her trip as he drove toward the Ocean Breeze and, once there, lost no time in heading for the restaurant where Bill and Madeline were waiting. Both of them got up when Tracy and Greg came near, and the women embraced.

'Welcome back,' Madeline said.

'It's good to be home.'

Tracy and Greg took seats at the

table, a waiter appeared and they all ordered dinner. Madeline wanted to know how Tracy's mother was doing, and she filled her in, saying nothing, however, about Paul. Finally, when they were midway through the meal, Tracy was able to bring up the subject of the Island Sands.

'What's happening there? Is the insurance problem settled yet?'

No one spoke for a moment, and Tracy put down her fork. 'Since you're not talking, I assume this means bad news.'

'I'm afraid so,' Bill said. 'I've called them almost every day and all I get is a big runaround. They say they're working on the problem, but nothing happens.'

'What is there to work on?' Tracy asked. 'Do they believe they insured you or not?'

'It turns out to be more complicated than that. They encountered a few Y2K problems — even though their system had been updated completely in 1999.'

'Just our luck,' said Madeline wryly. 'The whole world manages to escape the millennium bug — but not us.'

'Well, there were some shutdowns here and there,' Greg pointed out.

Madeline put down her fork, as if the topic of her hotel problems had taken away her appetite. 'Apparently a lot of their financial records vanished into cyberspace and no one knows how much money they have or where it is. Until they get it fixed, the computer won't let them write checks.'

'What about the bank?' Greg asked. 'Do they know about this problem? Can't they give you an interim loan so you can get started with the renovation?'

'Make that two companies dragging their feet,' Bill said.

Tracy felt as if her words were exploding. 'But they *can't* do that! Don't they realize how important it is for you to get the hotel back in shape?'

'If they do, it isn't bothering them much,' Bill said.

'Did you have the structure checked out and get all the estimates you needed?' Greg asked.

'Of course. But between their highly tuned aptitude for procrastination and a loan officer who seems to have developed a keen dislike for us, I can't get them to admit they've even looked at all the paperwork we submitted, much less make a commitment for a loan.'

Madeline reached over and put her hand over Bill's. In a low, quavering voice she said, 'They say we're not qualified. We don't have enough income.'

'Well, of course you don't right now,' Tracy said. 'But the hotel was doing fine before the tidal wave, and it will generate plenty of income after it's repaired. Besides,' she added, remembering something Madeline had said before the wedding, 'now that you and Bill are married, you should have an even better credit rating.'

Bill guffawed, indicating his disgust. 'Guess what? They called Chicago and found out I had resigned as manager of this hotel. So they've decided I have no income and I'm a poor credit risk!'

Tracy felt her cheeks grow hot and tears spring to her eyes. How could they do this? It was so unfair! 'But you've been manager while I've been away. You're still being paid, aren't you?'

'Sure, but that doesn't seem to matter to the bankers.'

'Damn!' Greg exploded. 'Sometimes, the way they throw up barriers, I swear banks are in the business of *not* lending money to people!'

'What about your inheritance?' Tracy asked. 'Doesn't that count for something?'

'We're using it to pay bills and pay a skeleton crew at the hotel, but unless something happens soon, that will run out, too.'

'Oh, Madeline — ' Tracy said.

Madeline interrupted her. 'Don't. We didn't mean to drag you into our problems. Let's not talk about it anymore.'

17

Early the next morning, Tracy and Greg drove to the airport and caught a flight to Kauai, rented a car, and drove toward Waimea Canyon. Greg handed her a small guidebook and, as he steered the car along roads lined with tulip trees, heliconia, bougainvillea and oleander, Tracy occasionally read parts of it aloud.

When not reading, or actively looking at the gorgeous scenery they passed, her mind focused on the man sitting close beside her. After leaving Madeline and Bill the previous night, she had pleaded jet lag and retired to her room to catch up on sleep. He'd kissed her good night at her door, and she'd wanted to go on kissing him. She'd even thought of inviting him inside, but her better judgment prevailed.

She'd told Greg why a romance

between them was out of the question. First, there was her job. If Titan Industries didn't buy the Ocean Breeze, she'd go on living in Hawaii and Greg in Los Angeles. Even if his company bought the hotel, she had no intention of going back to the mainland. She'd fallen in love with the islands and wanted to stay there, even if she lost her job and ended up working as a chambermaid. Second, she'd told Paul that she didn't need a man to make her life complete; and yet, the sight of Greg at the airport had made her pulse race. The thought of never seeing him again made her heart ache.

Greg's voice intruded on her thoughts. 'Look at the orchids.'

She turned her head quickly to see a field full of small native orchids on slender stems. 'Oh, they're beautiful.'

'They don't call this the Garden Isle for nothing.'

'You've been to Kauai before, haven't you?'

'As you know, I came here to check

out a hotel for Titan, but that's all I did on that trip. I heard about the canyon and the Fern Grotto and didn't want to see them alone. You told me you hadn't been to this island, so I decided to share it with you.' He looked over at her and grinned.

'I've been to Maui and the Big Island,' she said, 'and they're both lovely, so I'm sure this one is, too. But didn't they have a terrible hurricane here a few years ago?'

'Hurricane Iniki,' Greg said, 'back in '92. It's mentioned in the guidebook. Anyway, as you can see, you wouldn't know it anymore. Everything grows so quickly here.' He paused and looked over at her, as if he knew what she was thinking.

'The Island Sands will recover from the tidal wave quickly, too. A lot of the vegetation has come back already. I whisked you away before you had a chance to go over and see the place, but you'll be surprised at how good it looks.'

'But the hotel building — ' Tracy started.

Greg interrupted her. 'Let's not think of that today. We're here to enjoy ourselves, and there's nothing we can do about Madeline's and Bill's insurance problems anyway.'

'I know, but — '

'Look at that map I bought, will you? I don't want to miss the turnoff to the canyon.'

Tracy unfolded the map lying on the seat between them and found the road they were traveling. 'We're not there yet.'

'Watch for Kokee Lodge,' he said. 'I think there's a restaurant there and I want to stop for lunch. It's almost noon.'

Greg was right about the restaurant, and when they entered the State Park, they headed there first. An hour later, after a soup and sandwich lunch, they drove the Waimea Canyon Road to the Canyon lookout. When they left the car and walked to the railing at the rim, the view took Tracy's breath away. A yawning chasm met her gaze, a deep gorge surrounded by uneven jagged cliffs of green, blue and reddish-brown.

'Great isn't it?' Greg said. 'They call it the Grand Canyon of the Pacific.'

'It's spectacular. I had no idea.'

'You've seen the Grand Canyon in Arizona, of course.'

She turned to him. 'You'll think I'm an awful hick, but no, I'm never been there.'

Greg took her hand in his and grinned. 'Then I'll take you sometime.'

The thought of future excursions with him set her heart pounding again but she tried to concentrate on the incredible sight before them. Next, Greg led her down a path to other lookout points. After pulling a small camera out of the car's glove compartment, he took pictures of her against the magnificent backdrop of waterfalls and rock formations that changed color into pinks and purples with the shifting sun.

Their next stop was the Kalalau lookout into the canyon and the Alakai jungle. They made a brief stop in the Natural History museum, and then Greg declared it was time to start back. 'It's an hour and a half to Lihue. We still have to see the Fern Grotto.'

The Grotto was three miles down the Wailua River and could be reached only by a boat ride. A group was leaving to go up the river just as Greg and Tracy parked the car at the river dock, and they were fortunate to find two empty seats in the small craft. As the boat navigated its way between walls of dense vegetation, Tracy felt as if she were in the middle of a jungle adventure film.

Twenty minutes later, Greg helped her from the boat, and they walked up the path to the Fern Grotto, a huge rock amphitheater draped in ferns and firecracker vines. Caressed by the tropical air filled with the scent of ginger blossoms, she breathed deeply.

What a heavenly place. In the shelter of the Grotto, a peaceful contentment spread through her body, and she felt as if she could stay there forever.

The boatman came ashore last and Tracy was surprised to see him holding a guitar. He made a short speech about the Grotto, then began to play his instrument and sing the *Hawaiian Wedding Song*. It was the second time she'd heard it, the first being at Madeline and Bill's wedding. The lovely melody stirred her heart and brought tears to her eyes. Would she — could she — ever hear those strains played for her and Greg?

Several couples nearby moved closer together, held hands, or put their arms around each other. Greg came to Tracy's side and put his arm around her waist, and she leaned against his broad chest.

When the song was over, he tilted her head up and kissed her gently on the lips. 'We'll come back here again someday,' he said, 'on our wedding anniversary.'

Tracy felt her pulse begin to race and she pushed him away, laughing a little shakily. She'd been deeply moved by the moment but she wasn't sure of her own feelings yet. Despite what he'd just said, she needed to be sure of his feelings, too.

'Talk about confidence,' she said, walking slowly toward a cascade of water at the back of the Grotto, 'you certainly have more than your share.'

'I can dream, can't I?'

'What makes you think that dream has a chance of coming true?'

He caught up to her and grabbed her hand, turning her about to face him. 'Why not that one?'

'Because we still live in different worlds, that's why.' She pulled her hand free. 'Please, Greg. Let's not talk about that today. I told you I'm not interested in a long-distance relationship.'

'You were in Chicago for a long time.

Did you see that old boyfriend of yours again?'

Tracy felt her face grow hot and didn't speak for a moment. But the longer she paused, the more Greg would think she had something to hide. 'As a matter of fact, I did see him.'

'So is it on again with him?' The tone of his voice changed; he sounded bitter. 'Didn't you just say you didn't care for long-distance relationships? Chicago is a helluva lot farther from Hawaii than Los Angeles is.'

Before Tracy could reply to that, he continued, 'Or is he going to do what I can't: move out here to be with you?'

'No,' Tracy said, so sharply that several people nearby turned their heads. 'No,' she repeated softly. 'He's not moving here and I'm not moving back there. There's nothing between us anymore.'

'Are you sure? No regrets?'

'No regrets.'

Greg moved closer to her again, and seemed about to put his arms around her when the boatman blew his whistle to call them back to the shore. She hurried to obey, glad she didn't have to talk about her meeting with Paul and why she knew it was over between them.

They were silent on the boat ride back down the river, and silent again for some time as Greg drove to the airport for their flight back to Oahu.

Finally he said, 'You don't have to tell me anything. It's none of my business, I know; but I'm glad you aren't holding a torch for that guy. Maybe you don't think you and I could ever come together, but at least I don't have any competition at the moment.'

'I told myself a long time ago that I wouldn't depend on any man for my happiness, and I meant that. I love working in a hotel and my goal is still to manage a large one someday.'

She felt her stomach muscles tighten. She wasn't saying this well at all. Her resolve to never let a man into her life had begun to unravel, and the beautiful song she's heard still rang in her head. But her tone of voice apparently had convinced Greg that there was no point in continuing that conversation, for he didn't say any more on the subject, and soon they reached Lihue, returned the rental car and headed for the airline terminal.

As they sat in the waiting area, Tracy's thoughts drifted back to the Island Sands and what would happen to Madeline and Bill. Her friend had once confessed she worried she might lose the hotel, and now that seemed even more likely.

Greg interrupted her gloomy thoughts. 'You're frowning. Was it something I said?'

She turned toward him. 'No. I'm just worried about Madeline's hotel. I feel so helpless. If only there was something I could do.'

Greg's tone was teasing. 'You could lend them half a million bucks.'

'Or *you* could,' she countered.

And then a thought came to her.

Someone else could lend them half a million dollars. Titan Industries!

'Greg,' she said, leaning close and speaking softly. 'I have an idea. Why couldn't Titan Industries lend them the money?'

He paused a moment. 'Titan isn't in the business of lending money. They buy — '

'They buy hotels, I know. But don't they also invest in hotels? Why couldn't they choose the Sands?'

Greg shrugged. 'Since you put it that way, I suppose they could. But why would they want to?'

'Because you could convince them. They sent you out here to find investments for them. You could point out that an investment in the Sands would really pay off in the future. Not to buy it, of course,' she added, 'because Madeline and Bill want to keep it, but just give them enough capital to restore the place until the insurance money comes in.'

'But — ' he began.

She hurried on. 'Hawaiian banks may be slow and shortsighted, but Titan didn't get to be a big company by missing opportunities. And this could be a great opportunity for them.'

Greg laughed. 'I should send you to L.A. to champion the cause. You're very persuasive.'

'Does that mean that I've persuaded you to do it?'

'That means I'll try.'

Tracy leaned closer still and planted a kiss on Greg's cheek. 'Thank you.'

'Hey, not that I don't like being thanked with a kiss; but remember, this may not work. As we've already said, they *buy* hotels. And even when they just invest in them, they usually take control and run things their way. Maybe Madeline and Bill won't like the terms.'

'You may be right, but we'll cross that bridge when we come to it. Meanwhile, I just have a feeling that this is the answer. And I know you'll be able to persuade your boss to do it.'

Greg sighed. 'And after I've pulled off that miracle, maybe I can pull off an even bigger one.'

'Such as?'

'Such as persuading you to fall in love with me.'

18

Tracy didn't need to comment on Greg's statement because the terminal intercom came to life with an announcement that their flight would be delayed for two hours.

Tracy groaned. 'Two hours? What are we supposed to do in the meantime?'

'We could go over to the Hawaii Haven Hotel and have a mai tai. It's the hotel I came to look at for Titan, and it's very glamorous. I'd like to show it to you.'

'You mean before Titan buys it and destroys the glamour?' Tracy said it with a grin, and Greg laughed.

'Right.' He pulled her gently from the seat and they walked out of the terminal.

The sun was lower in the sky, but the air was still hot and a little humid. They reached their destination after a three-block walk. Greg had been right; the hotel was posh, with shiny glass and chrome doors that whispered open as they approached, walls of pale pink, floors of marble, and lots of exotic plants in enormous pots.

Greg propelled her through the lobby where their footsteps were hushed by a thick, pale-green carpet. Then he pointed out a formal dining room, and boutiques selling the latest fashions. Through more glass doors, he showed her the serpentine swimming pool with waterfalls and finally led her down a corridor to another body of water separated into indoor and outdoor sections by huge sliding glass doors. Waiting at the bottom of a short flight of stairs that led to the water was a small canopied boat.

'At night,' Greg told her, 'you can ride in the boat to go to one of three waterfront restaurants.'

'Wow,' Tracy said. 'This *is* glamorous.'

'There's more.' He took her arm and led her down another long corridor, then opened a door on the left revealing a large meeting room with a bar at the far end, and stacks of folding chairs.

'Whoops, wrong room,' Greg said.

He started to pull her back, when Tracy spied a long sofa against a nearby wall. 'Wait. Let's sit down for a moment. I feel like I've been walking miles.'

Greg led her to the sofa. 'I'm sorry. I guess the hotel is farther from the terminal than I realized. I shouldn't have made you walk so much. We'll take a cab back.'

They had no sooner seated themselves, when the door opened behind them. They heard a few footsteps and then the overhead lights suddenly switched off and the door closed again. A latch clicked. They were locked in the room, sitting in the dark.

Tracy began to laugh softly. 'I guess whoever that was didn't see us.'

'We're not supposed to be here.' Still, he made no move to get up. 'If we pounded on the door, he might come back and let us out.'

She didn't answer.

He reached for her hand and brought it to his lips. 'On the other hand, we could consider this to be fate stepping in. Now I have you all to myself. This is better than the Fern Grotto.'

Tracy left her hand in his. She felt her face begin to warm and her heartbeat quicken.

Greg caressed the smooth hair that fell back from her temples, letting his fingers sift down through the blond strands to her shoulders. His palms were hard, but not rough, as they slid slowly down her arms, prickling her flesh and spreading a driving warmth into the most sensitive parts of her body. She felt herself respond to him, deeply aroused although he had barely touched her.

As if he knew her thoughts, he lowered his mouth and kissed first her cheek, then her chin, gently, unhurriedly, more with a sense of exploration than urgency. She liked that, very much, and moved closer to him.

His next kiss was a passionate one, and his arms encircled her completely, holding her tight. She pulled him close, her hands pressing his back, sliding to his neck and up into his glossy, thick hair.

Pushed against the back of the sofa, she felt herself slip sideways. Almost at once they were lying on the sofa cushions, his body over hers, his chest pressing against her breasts, his kisses fevered and passionate.

Although he broke the kiss, he kept his mouth near hers. 'I didn't pay that person to lock us in, you know.'

'I know,' she whispered.

'But it's such a good idea.'

'I know,' she said again.

'Do you also know that I want you very much right now?'

'I can guess.'

He raised up slightly, looking down at her. Since her eyes had adjusted to the gloom, she could see him faintly.

'I don't just want you, Tracy — I'm

in love with you.'

She didn't answer; she couldn't. She wanted him, too. She wanted to feel his naked body against hers, to lose herself in passion and desire. He kissed her again, and she kissed him back with a fervor she didn't know she possessed. His mouth opened over hers, his tongue exploring. She felt her body arch into his.

'Tracy, Tracy,' he murmured. 'Do we have to catch that plane? You must tell me right now.'

She heard herself say, 'There'll be another plane.'

Moments later, clothing removed, they lay flesh against flesh. Her nails dug slightly into his back, her teeth nipped gently at his shoulders. He caressed her hips, kissed her breasts, sending flames into the deepest recesses of her body. Finally, at long last, drenched in a sweet sweat, they reached a climax that was like exploding fireworks.

★　★　★

Much later, they dressed and Greg used the telephone he found in the room to get someone to come and unlock the door. He changed their flight reservations and then requested a room in the hotel. Once again, Tracy forgot her doubts and let him make love to her.

They caught the first flight to Honolulu the next morning and went straight to the Ocean Breeze hotel, where they persuaded Madeline and Bill to join them for coffee on the patio.

Tracy began to tell them her idea that Greg should persuade Titan to invest in the Island Sands, but they reacted with extreme skepticism.

'They won't be interested,' Bill said firmly.

'But they might be,' Tracy insisted. 'Greg can convince them.'

'But even if they want to give us some money,' Madeline said, 'what kind of terms would they want? You told me that if Titan invests in the Ocean Breeze, they'll want to kick you out as manager.'

'That's not a given,' Greg said. 'They don't always do that.'

'But what if they wanted to take control of the Sands?'

'Well,' Greg pointed out, 'if you don't like the terms, you don't have to accept.'

Madeline leaned across the table toward Greg, lowering her voice, but speaking with great intensity. 'I can't give up the management of this hotel,' she said. 'You don't understand. My father bought it when my mother died over ten years ago and I've lived here ever since. This isn't just a job to me, it's my life.'

She ended on a plaintive note and, once again, Tracy felt especially close to Madeline, almost as if these problems were *her* problems, too.

After a small silence, Bill spoke up. 'A loan would sure help out; but if the local banks won't do it — '

'They do everything too slowly out here,' Greg said. 'I'm not encouraging you to think Titan will give you a loan, but *if* they saw the benefit and decided to do it, they'd move on it a lot faster.'

Madeline continued to frown and look worried. 'You have to convince them that it is just a loan. I'd never give up control of the Sands. Why, this place was built before World War II. It's not just old, it's historic. It survived the bombing of Pearl Harbor and two presidents have stayed here; I have clippings and letters — ' She stopped abruptly, looked down and put her hand up to her eyes.

Tracy knew why. Madeline was remembering that she no longer had any newspaper clippings or letters, not since the tsunami thundered through her office, smashed open the filing cabinet and ruined — if not washed away — every detail of the previous fifty-some years.

Greg looked at Madeline and spoke softly. 'I know what you want, and I'll do my best to get it for you.'

Tracy felt as if her own tears would start. She touched Greg's arm, grateful for his help.

He squeezed her hand in return and then, after another pause, pushed back his chair and got to his feet. 'I'm sorry to break this up, but my weekend was over last night and I have a plane to catch.'

Tracy rose, too. 'I'll walk back with you.' She turned and gave Madeline a hug.

Greg shook hands with both Madeline and Bill. 'Once more, believe me when I say I'll do my best for you.' Then he led Tracy from the patio to the doors of the lobby and then to his rental car.

As they stood together in the parking lot, she turned to him. 'You're leaving again and there's still so much to say.'

'I'll be back. I love you.'

'I — I want to believe you, but — in spite of last night — I seem to have doubts about myself.' Doubts about him too, and the possible folly of their actions.

'Well, it'll be different this time,' Greg said firmly. 'That guy in Chicago apparently rejected you for some reason. I'm not that kind of a fool. If we should break up, it would be because you want it, not me.'

'You're awfully sure of yourself.'

'I can't help it. I feel something so strong. It's like you're the other half of me and I never knew it was missing until I met you.'

He kissed her and stroked her back, murmuring softly into her hair, 'Oh, Tracy, I've been waiting for you all my life. I want to marry you.'

She didn't answer and he went on. 'I'm not looking for a replacement. I didn't come here for that, and I didn't expect to find it. But almost from the moment I saw you, I felt I'd been given a second chance at happiness, and I don't want to throw it away if I can help it.'

Once again, Tracy didn't know how to respond. And there was no time to explore her feelings now. 'You'd better hurry or you'll miss your flight.'

★ ★ ★

Greg telephoned her from the airport before getting on his plane back to Los Angeles, and again that night from his apartment, both times telling her that he loved her and couldn't wait until they could be together again.

She didn't repeat his words, and after a moment, he came right out and asked her, 'Do you love me, Tracy?'

'I — I don't know. I loved being with you last night, I know that much. But I need some time to sort out my feelings. I told you that Hawaii casts a spell over people. I accused you of succumbing to it, but perhaps I'm bewitched myself.'

'Well, if it's time you need, I guess we'll have enough of that — too much probably — because after that talk with my boss tomorrow I'm off on another business trip, this time to London.'

'Is Titan thinking of buying a hotel there, too?'

'They already own one. I have to settle a problem.'

'You seem to wear a lot of different hats. You scout out new property, you help build or remodel hotels, and then you make sure everything runs smoothly.'

'Seems that way, doesn't it? I've always liked the variety before. But right now, it's not so appealing. I want to spend all my time with you.'

'I'll tell you this much,' Tracy said. 'I know I'm going to miss you.'

'I'm glad to hear it. Hold the thought.' He paused for a moment, then said, 'I'd love to go on talking to you like this all night, but I have to get some sleep. I want to be at my best, my most persuasive, tomorrow morning when I try to talk Titan into investing in the Sands.'

They said good night and Tracy replaced the receiver and stretched out on her bed, remembering their lovemaking. From somewhere deep within her, she sighed.

19

Two weeks later, as Tracy was paying monthly bills in her office, she received a telephone call from Matthew Westphal. She was surprised to hear his voice, as he usually asked for Bill Griffin, not her.

'Hi, Tracy. Westphal here. The switchboard operator can't seem to find Bill. Do you know where he is?'

Tracy supposed he might be with Madeline at the Sands, but hated to say so in case their boss thought Bill was spending too much time over there. She didn't want to get him in trouble. He had asked to be kept on at the Ocean Breeze, but he spent several hours a day with Madeline, helping with the landscaping chores, now that they'd had to let their regular gardeners go.

'Why, I imagine he's out on the grounds somewhere. I'll be glad to hunt him down for you.'

'Do that. In the meantime, though, maybe you know something about what's going on.'

'Is something going on?'

Westphal's voice turned gruff. 'As you very well know, I've been trying to negotiate a deal with Titan Industries to buy the Ocean Breeze. Their man gave it a good report, or so I thought. And now, suddenly, indications are they're not buying it after all.'

Tracy couldn't help thinking this was good news, not bad, at least for her. 'I'm sorry, Mr. Westphal. Have they chosen something on another island or changed their minds about expanding in the Pacific?'

'No, they're going to buy the Island Sands instead.'

Tracy's thoughts swirled around in her head. Westphal must have misunderstood. Titan wasn't buying the Sands, they were just going to invest some money. But since Westphal already knew, that must mean Greg had been successful in persuading Titan. She felt her lips turn up in a grin.

Westphal wasn't finished, however, and his tone of voice became even louder and more unpleasant. 'What the hell have you and Bill been telling that Titan guy about the Ocean Breeze? What did you do that turned him off?'

Pleased though she was to know the Sands would be saved, she didn't like the idea that Westphal was angry. When she'd asked Greg to persuade Titan to invest in the Sands, she hadn't thought of what that might mean to Westphal's obvious desire to sell the Ocean Breeze. Now she felt ambivalent: On the one hand she had helped a friend; on the other she might seem like a traitor to her boss. But she hadn't meant to. She had never said anything derogatory about the Breeze and she was pretty sure that Bill hadn't either.

'Mr. Westphal,' she said, 'I'm terribly sorry, but we really — ' She stopped, unable to think of what she should say. 'Let me find Bill and have him call you back right away.'

'Do that.' The sound of the receiver banging down made Tracy's ear hurt.

She felt like a coward but maybe, given a little time to think about his response, Bill could come up with answers that would calm Westphal. But before she could act on that, the phone rang again.

This time it was Madeline. 'They're foreclosing!' she said, her voice shrill. 'The bank is foreclosing on us!'

Madeline's words made no sense. Westphal had just said Titan was saving them. The bank couldn't foreclose now. She jumped up from her chair. 'Is Bill with you?'

'No,' Madeline said. 'I asked for him first, but the switchboard didn't know where he was.'

'I'll find him,' Tracy said, 'and have him call you right away.'

After Tracy found Bill and told him about Westphal's message, he didn't call Madeline. Instead, he decided to go straight to the Sands and talk to her in person. Tracy tagged along, hoping to find out what was going on.

When the three of them were settled in Madeline's office, she repeated that she'd received a letter in the mail announcing that the bank was exercising their right to call her loan, and that she had only two weeks to pay the outstanding balance or they would begin foreclosure proceedings.

'I don't understand,' Madeline said, her words coming in spurts as she tried to control her emotions, 'they drag their feet on everything and now, suddenly, they move to foreclose — like a tornado!'

Bill took the paper from Madeline's hands and read it silently, then took her in his arms and hugged her, planting kisses on her forehead and hair. 'It's all a mistake. You know how this bank operates. The left hand never knows what the right hand is doing.'

'But — '

'Don't worry,' he repeated. 'I'm going over there right now and get it all straightened out.' He turned to Tracy. 'I'll call Westphal as soon as I can.' He paused. 'By the way, have you heard anything from Greg about Titan lending us the money? Why did Westphal know before we did?'

'I don't know. Greg's been in London, and hasn't called for several days.' She stood up. 'But I'll put a call through to him right away and tell him it's urgent that he get back to me.' She opened her purse and took out her telephone credit card.

★ ★ ★

But Greg didn't call that day, nor the next. Tracy left another message, and then another. Her rising sense of panic threatened to strangle her. What was going on? Why didn't he call?

Meanwhile, she learned that Bill had spoken with the loan officer, who insisted he knew nothing about an offer from Titan and was just doing his job. The head office wanted them to start foreclosure proceedings and that's what they were doing.

By the third day, Tracy considered calling Titan Industries herself to ask about the loan. She had their telephone number from Greg. But she didn't know who to ask for or what to say. It wasn't even her hotel that needed the money. Tracy was about to suggest Bill call Titan directly, but before she could act on that impulse, Bill came into her office and sat on the chair in front of her desk. His face was drawn, his shoulders slumped.

'What is it?' she asked. 'Have you heard something?' Judging by his expression, if he had heard anything, it wasn't good news.

He looked straight at Tracy and spoke softly. 'Titan Industries is buying the Sands.'

Tracy began to feel relieved. 'Then they finally know about the loan.'

'You don't understand. This is not a loan. I mean they're buying it.' He took a deep breath before continuing. 'I went to the bank again and talked to their highest officer. I told them about Westphal knowing Titan was giving us the loan and demanded to know why they kept insisting on foreclosure. They finally told me.'

'And — ?'

'They've had an offer from Titan to buy the hotel *after* they foreclose on us.'

Tracy could hardly believe her ears. 'I don't believe it.'

'They made an offer the bank couldn't refuse.'

'But Titan was going to give you a loan.'

'Apparently not. Greg never told you they agreed to that, did he?'

'No, but — '

Bill went on. 'The officer told me that Titan admitted they had narrowed their search for a Hawaiian hotel to the Ocean Breeze, but when they found out the Sands was in big financial trouble, they decided to drop the offer on the Breeze and pick up the Sands at a bargain price instead.'

Tracy felt her face get hot, her chest tighten, her legs tremble. This could mean only one thing: Gregory Thompson, the man who said he loved her — even asked her to marry him — had betrayed them. He must have told Titan they could get the Sands in foreclosure.

'Oh, Bill,' she said. 'I'm so sorry. It's all my fault. If I hadn't suggested to Greg — '

Bill reached across the desk and took Tracy's hand. 'You couldn't know this would happen.'

Tears sprang to her eyes. Greg had destroyed Madeline and Bill's dreams, their very life. 'I thought he'd ask for the loan. Instead he . . . he betrayed us — he told them the Sands would be a bargain in foreclosure. That's why they did it.'

'You don't know that for sure,' Bill said.

Tracy took a deep breath and clenched her jaw. Speaking through tight, drawn lips, she said, 'Oh, yes, I do. That explains why he hasn't returned my calls. What a fool I was to trust him . . . '

With a final pat on her arm, Bill got up and left her office.

When he'd gone, Tracy put her head down on her desk and gave way to weeping. How could Greg do this to her, just when she had finally admitted to herself that she loved him?

★ ★ ★

Two nights later, as Tracy prepared for bed, her telephone rang.

'Hello, my love.' It was Greg. Tracy's knees started to tremble the moment she heard his voice and she had to sit down on the edge of the bed.

'I've missed you,' he said, 'but I'm finally back in Los Angeles. As soon as I get a chance, I'm going to fly over to see you again. Titan owes me a couple of days off.'

She'd rehearsed in her mind at least a dozen times what she'd say if she ever heard from him again, how she'd

250

accuse him of betrayal, how she'd call him every vile name her brain could imagine. But now the words refused to come out.

'Tracy? Are you all right?'

She tried to keep her voice calm. 'Yes, I'm all right. That is, as right as I can be when I've had to watch my best friend lose everything that ever mattered to her and know that I'm responsible because I trusted *you*.' She said the last word loudly.

'Me? What have I done? What's this all about?'

'You told Titan Industries that they could pick up the Island Sands in foreclosure.'

'I did what?'

'You heard me. The bank is foreclosing on Madeline, and Bill found out that it's because Titan offered them a deal if they'd foreclose.'

'Titan offered . . . But that can't be true.'

Tracy took a deep breath. 'Congratulations. You're quite a good actor. You make it sound as if you knew nothing about this.'

'But I didn't. I don't! I told Titan exactly what you asked me to. I suggested they give Madeline and Bill a loan until the insurance company pays up or the hotel restoration is complete. I pointed out the superior location of the Sands, its history, the dedication of the two owners — '

'I'm not as naive you seem to think I am. The truth is that you work for the company and you put their interests ahead of everything else — '

His voice turned steely. 'Is that the kind of man you think I am?'

'I suppose I shouldn't blame you. After all, you just did what was expected of you. You'll probably get a bonus for giving them this opportunity, at least a big finder's fee.'

'Tracy, stop it right now. I'm telling you the truth. I had nothing to do with any foreclosure or Titan making an offer for the hotel.'

'Tell your lies to someone else. I'm

not buying them.'

'I'm flying out to see you on the first plane I can get.'

'Don't bother. I never want to see you again.'

20

Greg flew to Hawaii anyway. There wasn't time to stop at the office and speak to his boss personally; but he left a message in his voice mail and reminded him of his cell phone number. Then he boarded the first flight to Honolulu.

This time the balmy air, the scent of tropical flowers, the blue sky and even bluer water of the islands failed to lift his spirits. All he could think of, as he drove to the Ocean Breeze, was that Tracy thought he was guilty of betraying her best friends. He had to tell her the truth and try to help undo whatever it was she thought he'd done.

But first he wanted to know the facts. Instead of going straight to Tracy's office, he stopped in the hotel lobby and placed a call from the public phones to Andrew Varney at Titan. But

Varney had already left the office. Greg threw himself into one of the lobby chairs. What should he do now? Wait until he could talk to his boss, or just go ahead and confront Tracy?

The matter was taken out of his hands when he saw her cross the lobby on the way to the elevators. He jumped up and followed her, catching up just as she pushed the button. The doors opened, she got in, and he did the same, immediately pushing the button for the roof level.

Tracy's eyes widened, then narrowed, as did her mouth. 'You! How can you even show your face here after what you've done?' She punched the Open Door button, but the elevator had already begun to rise.

'I've done nothing.' He put out his hands, palms up. 'Tracy, you've got to let me explain. If Titan has tried to buy the Sands, it's the first I know of it.'

'*If* they try to buy the Sands? There's no *if* about it; they've made an offer to the bank and the bank is foreclosing on

Madeline and Bill. You can do your explaining to them. If you dare,' she added.

'I swear to you I knew nothing about it. I tried to get them to invest some money, that's all. Then I got sent to London and I called you as soon as I got back.'

'Acting innocent, as if you didn't know anything.'

'I *don't* know anything. How could I?'

'You could have returned my calls. I left a dozen messages.'

'What calls? I never got any messages.' He felt his anger rising, but tried not to show it. He wasn't angry at *her*. It must have been the switchboard operator at the London hotel. Those things could happen even in the best of places. But it sounded like a lame excuse and he knew Tracy wouldn't believe it.

'No, of course not,' she was saying. 'You're totally innocent of everything.'

Her tone was slightly sarcastic, but he

felt he deserved her scorn. 'I am innocent, but I don't blame you for not understanding. If we could just sit down and talk — '

The elevator stopped and the doors opened at the roof level, but Tracy didn't get out. She punched the button for the second floor. 'Talk won't fix this.'

'I'm sorry if anything I said or did — '

'Being sorry won't help either.' The doors opened on the second floor and she moved hurriedly. 'Just leave me alone, do you hear?'

This time he didn't follow her. He let the doors close and then hit the first floor button. He'd find Madeline and Bill and talk to them. Maybe they would listen to him.

Madeline wasn't at the Ocean Breeze, but Bill took pity on him and ushered him into the restaurant for a cup of coffee. 'You've got to understand — ' Bill began.

Greg shrugged. 'I can't understand

anything when no one will talk to me.'

Bill poured coffee for them both and gestured to a small table in the corner of the room. Greg obeyed Bill's nod and sat down in one of the two chairs.

'What happened,' Bill said, 'was that first my boss, Matthew Westphal called, all upset because Titan wasn't buying the Ocean Breeze. He figured we'd blown the deal somehow.' He took a gulp of coffee before continuing. 'Before I could even talk to him about it, I found out the bank said they were calling the loan. I stormed over there and talked to the chief loan officer and he finally admitted that Titan had made them an offer that was a lot more than our balance.'

'How long ago was this?' Greg asked. 'What's the time frame?'

'We have to pay off the entire loan in — ' He paused, calculating. 'Five more days.'

Greg felt the hairs on the back of his neck rise. This was worse than he had imagined. 'And you can't.'

'No way.'

'Have you called any other banks, tried to get a swing loan?'

'There are only two banks on the whole island that will lend money on rental property, and the other one isn't interested. Ever since the Japanese financial crisis sent our tourism industry into a tail-spin, things have been really tight over here.'

Greg leaned forward. 'Bill, you've got to believe me — I had nothing to do with this. I told my boss just what you wanted me to say: that the Island Sands would be a good investment, that you and Madeline had your hearts in it as well as years of experience.'

'I believe you. I told Tracy it wasn't your fault. If we're going to assign blame we could start with Madeline's father, who left her with a mortgage that should have been paid off long ago.' He shrugged. 'It's only business. You said we needed the money, so Titan did their own investigating and figured out a way to get the whole pie instead of just a piece of it.'

'I can't tell you how sorry I am.'

'Don't. I understand. I learned a long time ago you can never go wrong overestimating the greed of corporate America.'

'I know what you mean,' Greg said, 'but let's not condemn everyone. I'd like to think there are still a few ethical businessmen in the world.'

'Yeah, you're right. Until now, Matthew Westphal has been an okay guy. First I resigned as manager of the Breeze and then I had to ask him for my job back and he reinstated me.'

'Will you and Madeline be okay?'

'Sure. Aside from Madeline losing the hotel her father left her, the only bad thing is that Tracy lost her opportunity to take over as manager here. She's qualified, but I need the job myself now.'

'I told Tracy I could probably find her a job in Los Angeles, but she wasn't keen to leave Hawaii. And now — '

'Judging from what I've heard and

what Madeline's told me, she hates your guts.'

'And every other part of me.' He swallowed some coffee. 'You see, it's not just the loan — '

Bill interrupted him. 'Yeah, I gather you two finally made beautiful music together and apparently that makes it worse'

'I do love her, you know.'

'Then give it time, she'll get over this. Eventually she'll realize Titan Industries would have screwed us anyway and there's nothing you can do to stop it.'

Greg pushed his cup aside and stood up. 'I can try to stop it, anyway.'

* * *

For the second time in less than twenty-four hours, Greg boarded a plane for the 2,300-mile journey. He told himself he was racking up lots of frequent-flyer miles, but that was small consolation for the pain in his head and the knot in his gut. And just what was he going to do in Los Angeles? He'd told Bill he was going to try to stop Titan, but that had been just bravado. He almost blushed, remembering his well meant words. As if he really could do anything. He turned out his reading lamp, closed the shade at his window and tried to get some sleep. Maybe a brilliant idea would come to him from his subconscious. Yeah, right.

At precisely nine the next morning, Greg went to see Andrew Varney. His office occupied a corner of the twentieth floor of the Titan Building on Wilshire Boulevard, with floor-to-ceiling windows, richly paneled walls and grass green carpeting thick enough to hide golf balls.

Varney sat behind his walnut desk. His coat was off, but he hadn't loosened the red and navy blue striped tie at his neck, nor rolled up the sleeves of his spotlessly white shirt. His gray hair made a frizzy ring around his tan bald spot and his green eyes were bright behind his glasses. He spoke in his usual used-to-be-Southern accent. 'Mornin', Greg.'

Greg dispensed with formalities. 'You get my message?'

'Yep, you want to talk to me. What about?'

'About an offer to buy the Island Sands in Hawaii.'

'So?'

'Tell me straight, Andy. Did you call the bank that holds the mortgage and offer to buy the hotel if they'd foreclose?'

Varney didn't answer right away; his back seemed to get even straighter and his face took on a closed look. Greg could see that he was getting defensive.

'As I recall, you told me about the hotel yourself, said it was in trouble.'

'Yes, but I wanted you to invest in it, not buy it.'

'What the hell difference does it make whether I put in a quarter million or the whole ball of wax?'

'The difference is that the bank is going to foreclose on the owners so you can buy it.' He paused, trying not to let his voice rise too much. 'These are my friends, Andy. You've forced them to foreclose on my friends.'

Varney reached into the humidor on his desk for a cigar, took his time about clipping off the end and lighting it. Which was just as well, Greg thought, because he needed to get control of himself. He sat down in the leather chair in front of the desk and took a deep breath, loosening the tie that seemed about to choke him.

'Look, Greg,' Varney said, blowing a circle of smoke into the air, 'I'm sorry. I didn't know they were your friends, did I?'

'I'm sure I pointed out how important it was that you help these people.' Even as he spoke, he realized he'd been naive to think that mattered. 'At least you could have discussed it with me first.'

'You weren't here.'

'You sent me to London, not the edge of the galaxy. You could have reached me at any time.'

Varney paused some more, and Greg knew he'd gone too far.

Each word fell like a boulder off a cliff. 'I'm not in the habit of requiring advice from my subordinates before I make a business decision.' He puffed once on his cigar. 'You gave me the facts; I evaluated them and did what I thought was best for the company and the stockholders. That's my job.'

Greg felt his palms sweat. The guy might as well have added, 'And if you don't like it — ' He didn't like it, but he'd have to make one more try. He forced himself to keep well back in the chair, to relax his hands on the armrests. 'My original recommendation,' Greg said, 'was to put in a bid for the Ocean Breeze, a very nice piece of property at a price that Westphal is willing to negotiate. I think that's a better deal for the company in the long run. It sustained no damage from the tsunami that devastated the Island Sands.'

'That damage is the very reason the Sands is cheap. You know the way we work — we were going to modernize anyway. The tsunami just makes it easier.'

'That's my point. The Sands doesn't need to be modernized. It's a beautiful old building with charm and character. It withstood the bombing of Pearl Harbor. Two presidents have stayed there.'

'Presidents will like it better with modern plumbing.'

'Plumbing is one thing, but you have to promise not to tear out the grand staircase or — ' He stopped, wishing he'd bitten his tongue before he used the word 'promise.' What was he thinking? He knew better than this. His brain had obviously turned to mush.

Varney smiled. 'Take it easy, Greg. You do a good job and I don't want to lose you. But I'm still not taking orders from you or anyone else. Is that clear?'

Greg stood up, his fists clenched at

his sides, his voice low. 'You're determined to go ahead and force the bank to foreclose on my friends?'

'If that's what it takes. Friends are friends, business is business.'

'I'm sorry to have to say this, but I think you're behaving in an unethical manner.'

'You have a right to your opinion.'

Greg couldn't stop. 'Under those circumstances' — he took a breath that felt all too shallow — 'I have no choice but to resign.'

Varney knocked off the ash from his cigar into the onyx ashtray on the corner of the desk. 'I do what I must — you do what you must.'

Greg stayed still for another minute, staring at Varney's impassive face. Then he turned and walked to the door. When he'd gone through and closed it behind him, the reality of what he'd done hit him hard.

Great, he told himself. *You did just great!* He'd once told himself that he'd never let business come between him and a wife a second time, and now it had ruined any chance of that even before it began. Tracy would never marry him now . . . and he'd just talked himself out of a job.

21

Her arms laden with large, clear plastic bags filled with flower leis, Tracy hurried along the wooden dock at Honolulu harbor, her sandals making soft slapping sounds on the old timbers. Although it was barely seven o'clock, the sun was high and the air warm, filled with the scent of flowers, salt sea water and the diesel fuel from the tug she was about to board.

A gray-bearded old sailor in faded jeans stopped her. 'Where's yer pass?'

'I have it right here.' Momentarily setting down one of her bags, Tracy reached for the candy-striped cotton pouch that served as her purse. She pulled it open and searched for the card that gave her permission to board one of the tugs going to Diamond Head to meet the cruise ships.

Before she found it, the old man

recognized her. 'Oh, it's you, Miz Barnes. You go on ahead.'

Smiling at him, she retrieved her bag and continued on her way to the bobbing tugboat, where she was helped aboard by a very tanned dockhand in tight T-shirt and rolled-up white trousers. After thanking him, she sat down on a bench near the small wheelhouse.

Four other women had already boarded and stood in a circle near the railing. They were assistant managers from other Waikiki hotels, who were making the trip for the same reason. They waved to her and she waved back, but didn't get up to join them. Madeline — who'd made this trip with her in the past — was not among them, and Tracy wasn't in the mood to speak to anyone else this morning.

At that moment, the commotion on the dock increased, lines were cast off and the boat moved out into the harbor, accompanied by several screeching and swooping white-winged birds, which Tracy had not yet learned to identify. They resembled seagulls, but she'd been told there were no seagulls in Hawaii. She also noticed two other tugboats chugging along ahead of them. One, she knew, contained the pilot who would bring the cruise ship into Honolulu harbor.

She needed this quiet time to sort out her thoughts and try to make sense of what had happened in the past few days. Upset, and feeling guilty about the foreclosure on the Island Sands, she'd hardly dared to look at Bill and avoided Madeline.

Then suddenly, just yesterday, Madeline had come to her and said that a miracle had occurred. 'They're not foreclosing,' she'd said, clutching Tracy's arms in a painful grip. 'Titan isn't buying the Sands.'

'What? How?'

'They changed their minds.'

'I don't understand,' Tracy said. 'What made them change?'

'Bill says they want to buy the Ocean Breeze after all.'

'Bill never said a word to me.'

'I think he's waiting until he can talk to Westphal and make sure he still wants to sell.'

Tracy felt confused. Titan was not buying the Sands, so the bank was not foreclosing, but — 'Does this mean the bank is giving you more time to come up with the money, or did they put some pressure on the insurance company to pay up?'

'Guess what? The Hawaii Historical Society got into it.' Madeline's voice rose and she was almost jumping up and down with excitement. 'They heard about our hotel and decided it's a historical landmark and they want to help us save it.'

'Oh, Madeline, that's fantastic.' She'd hugged her friend and felt tears spring to her eyes. The nightmare was over. Madeline wouldn't lose her hotel after all. Not only that, but the wonderful old structure would be restored to its former grandeur, and lose none of its vintage charm. Dreams did come true.

Now, as the tugboat went farther out into the open waters, Tracy felt an urge to shed tears of joy. She shook her head and got up from the bench, pushing her flower bags underneath, and headed unsteadily for the railing. Looking forward, she could see ahead of the craft and feel the fresh air on her face. The breeze lifted her hair so that it floated just above her ears, and she crinkled her eyes into the brilliant sunlight dancing on the water.

'Did you take your seasickness pills?' she overheard one of the women ask another, and the answer was, 'Yes, I always do. I almost don't get into the bathtub without it.'

Tracy laughed and widened her stance to brace herself, clutching the worn wooden rail. An occasional wave splashed over the deck, drenching her bare legs and feet with salt water, but she didn't want to move. Now cruising close to the shore, the tugboat passed the many hotels lined along the beach and soon Diamond Head came into view, its majestic height dwarfing the highrises and giving her the same thrill she'd had when she'd viewed it for the first time. She knew the mountainous form at the eastern tip of Oahu was an extinct volcano and, unlike Kilauea or Mauna Loa on the big island, hadn't erupted for hundreds of years.

Her thoughts were interrupted by the sudden realization that they were approaching the cruise ship. She rushed to the starboard side of the tug, where a gigantic gleaming white ship was coming ever closer. Like a picture postcard, portholes lining the sleek sides, smokestacks leaning to the stern, shiny brightwork glinting with reflected sunlight, the sight thrilled her again.

The other women were already getting ready to transfer to the ship, and Tracy went back to the bench to retrieve her bags. Her euphoria began to melt; she hadn't made this trip to greet passengers staying at the hotel since the day she'd met Greg. Madeline had done the honors while Tracy was in

Evanston. Her stomach began to knot. Greg wouldn't be on the ship this time. She wouldn't see his smile, or the dark hair that always tumbled onto his forehead.

Stop this, she told herself. She wouldn't see Greg this time, or ever again. It was all over.

She sighed, got into line and climbed up the steps into the ship, then to the deck and the lounge where a table with the name of the hotel awaited her.

She'd greeted all of the hotel's guests by the time the ship was close to Aloha Tower, and she'd returned the remaining leis to one of the plastic bags and gotten ready to leave the lounge. Suddenly, a shadow came between her and the light from the huge open windows. She looked up, and Greg stood in front of her.

But it couldn't be him, this couldn't be happening. Her cheeks felt hot, her breath quickened and her heart began to pound. She couldn't speak.

He pulled out a circle of purple

plumeria from the bag on the table and held it up, grinning. 'Aren't you going to offer me a lei, like you did before?'

Still unsure what she should say or do, Tracy continued to stare, until Greg came around the table and put the lei around her neck.

'I'd kiss you,' he said softly, his voice a warm whisper near her ear, 'but I'm not sure how you'll respond. I don't want to get my face slapped in front of a dozen people.'

'I'm — I'm sorry,' she finally managed. 'I wanted to tell you that a long time ago. I know it wasn't your fault that Titan decided to buy the Sands, but when I called your company to apologize for my behavior to you, they said you no longer worked there.'

'That's right. At first I didn't know they'd convinced the bank to foreclose on the Sands so they could buy it. And then when I found out, I quit.'

'You quit your job because of — '

'Not just because of you, or Madeline and Bill. It was a question of integrity. I didn't want to be part of a company that could do something I considered underhanded.'

Tracy frowned. 'I'm so sorry. I didn't mean for it to cost you your job.'

He grinned. 'It's okay. I can get another one.'

She smiled back at him. What a remarkable person he was. She wanted to hug him right there, then remembered she had good news.

'Titan isn't buying the Sands. I just found out yesterday that they're buying the Ocean Breeze after all, and the Hawaii Historical Society is going to put up the money to save Madeline's hotel. Isn't that wonderful?'

'Great.' He took both her hands in his and looked deep into her eyes. 'So everything's all right now?'

'Oh, yes.' She paused, then added, 'Well, almost everything. With Titan buying the Breeze, Mr. Westphal told me they're bringing in their own management team. I guess I'm out of a job.' Then she remembered what he'd said. 'Correction, we're *both* out of a job right now.' She waited for some reaction to that, but saw none. He continued to smile.

'You once offered to find me a position in L.A. Is that still a possibility, or will you be taking any hotel job that comes along yourself?'

'No, I still want to help you. If that's what you really want.'

'I'd rather stay in Hawaii, but I guess that's impossible,' she said. 'I've been in the hotel business since I graduated from college. I don't think I'm qualified for some other field, even if I wanted to switch. Which I don't.'

His hands moved to her shoulders and he brought her close again. 'I was rather hoping you'd be interested in another career. Ever thought of becoming a wife?'

Tracy's heart beat faster. Had he really said *wife*? As in *his* wife? Her throat tightened and she didn't answer.

'Would you marry me, Tracy, even if I don't have a job?'